ABOUT THE AUTHOR

In May 1959, after spending a couple of years in the Rhodesia and Nyasaland Staff Corps, Jeremy Mallinson joined the staff of Gerald Durrell's newly formed zoological park in Jersey. During his forty-two-year career in zoos and conservation he has studied animals in Africa, Asia and South America.

He served as Gerald Durrell's Deputy and Zoological Director and, after his mentor's death in 1995, he was appointed Director of the renamed Durrell Wildlife Conservation Trust

He has written more than two hundred papers and articles, addressed conferences and meetings in over twenty different countries, and is the author of ten books. He has received many awards for his service to animal conservation worldwide, including a DSc (Hon) from the University of Kent and an OBE in 1997.

Jeremy Mallinson lives in Jersey.

BY THE SAME AUTHOR

Okavango Adventure – In Search of Animals in Southern Africa (David & Charles, 1973; W.W. Norton & Company Inc., New York, 1973)
Earning Your Living with Animals (David & Charles, 1975)
Modern Classic Animal Stories (David & Charles, 1977). Republished as: *Such Agreeable Friends – Adventures with Animals* (David & Charles, Vancouver, 1977)
The Shadow of Extinction – Europe's Threatened Wild Mammals (Macmillan, 1978)
The Facts About a Zoo (G. Whizzard, 1980)
Travels in Search of Endangered Species (David & Charles, 1989)
'Durrelliania' – An Illustrated Checklist (Bigwoods, 1999)
The Count's Cats, a novel (Llumina Press, 2004)
The Touch of Durrell – A Passion for Animals (Book Guild, 2009; in paperback, 2018)
Les Minquiers – Jersey's Southern Outpost (Seaflower Books, 2011; new edition: Seaflower Books, 2020)
Someone Wishes to Speak to You, a novel (Book Guild, 2014)

On the Subject of Relationships

Jeremy Mallinson

The Book Guild Ltd

First published in Great Britain in 2021 by
The Book Guild Ltd
9 Priory Business Park
Wistow Road, Kibworth
Leicestershire, LE8 0RX
Freephone: 0800 999 2982
www.bookguild.co.uk
Email: info@bookguild.co.uk
Twitter: @bookguild

Copyright © 2021 Jeremy Mallinson

The right of Jeremy Mallinson to be identified as the author of this
work has been asserted by him in accordance with the
Copyright, Design and Patents Act 1988.

All rights reserved. No part of this publication may be
reproduced, transmitted, or stored in a retrieval system, in any form or by any means,
without permission in writing from the publisher, nor be otherwise circulated in
any form of binding or cover other than that in which it is published and without
a similar condition being imposed on the subsequent purchaser.

Typeset in Minion Pro

Printed on FSC accredited paper
Printed and bound in Great Britain by 4edge Limited

ISBN 978 1913551 513

British Library Cataloguing in Publication Data.
A catalogue record for this book is available from the British Library.

For Brother Miles,
Who introduced me to the writings of my mentor,
Gerald Durrell,
Which led to my forty-two-year career with
'His Family and Many Other Animals'.

ACKNOWLEDGEMENTS

The book, which merges fact with fiction, has greatly benefited from the opportunities that I have had in life to travel extensively to many different countries in the world. And particularly, as far as this narrative is concerned, the many months I spent with Robert and June Kay, with their two pet lions, travelling around the Okavango Swamps in the Bechuanaland Protectorate (Botswana), during the winter of 1961/1962. For such an experience provided me with an excellent insight into the day-to-day lives of some of the local tribal people, as well as to the wonders of the country's wildlife heritage.

I am grateful to Rob Hillman for providing me with some observations of his time at Durham University. To Peter Stevens, for giving me an insight into how the British Colonial Police Service operated in the Bechuanaland Protectorate up to 1966. Also, to Peter and his wife, Vicky, for giving me some useful additional information about their time working in this part of southern Africa. I am also greatly indebted to Antony McCammon, for providing me with some excellent ideas and a significant amount of editorial comment. And to Imogen Palmer, who greatly developed the book's dialogue, fixed inconsistencies, and aided the reader to become more directly involved with its main characters. Also, in much appreciation for the valued help of the Book Guild's production team

PREFACE

This novel is a sequel to the author's *Someone Wishes to Speak to You*, which describes how the son of a British baronet, Mathew Duncan, a primatologist, became involved with the tragedies and ramifications of Southern Rhodesia's disastrous Bush War during the 1970s, whilst carrying out research in Southern Central Africa.

On the Subject of Relationships continues with a narrative that marries historical fact with the drama of fiction. Set in 2003, Mathew Duncan's son, Charles, an anthropologist, is studying for his doctorate degree on the culture and traditions of the Herero tribe in Southern Africa.

Before Charles's departure from Durham University to undertake his research in Botswana and Namibia, he is recruited by a visiting lecturer to become an informer for MI6. This brings him into contact with secret service agents attached to the British High Commissions operating in both countries. MI6 was at this time particularly interested in Chinese and Japanese mineral corporations who were competing to exploit the substantial mineral wealth of both countries. In some cases, these organisations were involved in clandestine dealings with subversive tribal elders and corrupt governmental officials to gain a monopoly of both countries' valuable mineral resources – and make a substantial profit at the expense of local communities.

On arrival in Botswana, Charles is welcomed into a local village as the guest of a tribal chief, and during his time there comes into contact with blackmail, witchcraft and murder. When his studies take him to Namibia it becomes clear how widespread the web of corruption has developed, and how far those involved are prepared to go to achieve what they require.

While studying at Durham University, Charles falls in love with fellow graduate, Christiane Lüneberg. Christiane joins him in Namibia, researching an aristocratic German ancestor, but is their future happiness as secure as Charles would like to believe?

Charles's investigations centre around the historical facts of the European colonisation in Africa, focussing particularly on the treatment of the Herero tribe by the German colonisers, committed after General Lothar von Trotha's 1904 'Order of Extermination'.

On returning from Africa, there is an unexpected twist in the tail, ending with an explosive revelation that could carry serious implications for Charles's future.

1

A CASE OF COINCIDENCE

Charles Duncan first came to the attention of Philip Eisenberg while he was in the process of completing the third year of his BA in Social Anthropology at Durham University. Eisenberg, an Honorary Research Fellow, was aware that Charles was an exceptional student, and that he intended to study the sociology of the Herero people in Botswana and Namibia, two countries that were currently of significant interest to his former employers.

Prior to Eisenberg arriving at Durham University, he had spent over thirty-five years in a number of different junior and senior appointments with the British government's Secret Intelligence Service (SIS), otherwise known as MI6. During his career he had operated in countries as diverse as Portugal, Madagascar, Brazil, Zimbabwe, Nepal, Sri Lanka and the Democratic Republic of the Congo.

Philip Eisenberg had studied French, Portuguese and mathematics at the University of Edinburgh where, in his final year of study, he had been approached by an SIS talent spotter. At that time it was standard practice for MI6 to trawl through the student lists at UK universities, to seek potential recruits from among the most intelligent and adventurous of the young academics. SIS favoured this method of recruitment, for potential candidates could be easily assessed and interviewed. This process was relatively risk-free, operationally straightforward and cost effective.

At the time of Eisenberg's selection and subsequent employment by the Intelligence Service, the SIS had only comparatively recently evolved from being a self-selecting and self-perpetuating gentleman's club with the majority of its members having been recruited from the environments of a public school and Oxbridge.

After Eisenberg had retired from the senior ranks of the SIS, he joined Durham University as a Research Fellow. His Secret Intelligence Service background was not public knowledge. Rather, it was put about that he had served in a number of different places around the world in a senior capacity in the UK Diplomatic Corps and was to undertake a series of tutorials about his work and operational skills.

So, history had almost repeated itself, in that Eisenberg had in turn been requested by SIS to keep an eye open for the type of high-achieving student who might be encouraged, in one capacity or another, to help with intelligence-gathering. In particular, if they were likely to become involved in business or research projects overseas.

Those running the SIS well recognised how graduates with proven intellectual prowess and minds full of curiosity could be ideally placed to collect important data from the local inhabitants of regions of special interest to the Foreign & Commonwealth Office (FCO). As the information source would have a good operational cover with his or her business or research projects, they could be in an excellent position to collect and convey valuable information, with little danger that their secret activities might be betrayed. Of course, if they were found out, the consequences could potentially be dire. Such important first-hand information about local opinions and conditions could provide valuable input in helping to guide the UK government's wide range of political, commercial, security and economic issues, all in pursuit of Great Britain's national interests.

Charles was an obvious candidate. Eisenberg had been conducting some research of his own and had found no skeletons in the cupboard here, nothing that wouldn't indicate a young man of good character with a bright future ahead of him. Although far from arrogant, Charles had a reassuring air of confidence. He looked slightly older than his twenty-one years, tall and dark with undeniable good looks. He was exceptionally bright and focussed on his studies; Charles ticked all the boxes.

Charles Duncan had first been introduced to Philip Eisenberg at a small gathering organised by his tutor, Professor Sam Prior. Less than two weeks later, while Charles was walking out of his college of St Hild and St Bede, he had been surprised when Eisenberg had come up to him, grasped his hand and said, 'After meeting you the other evening at Professor Sam Prior's, he told me that you are a son of a former acquaintance of mine, Dr Mathew Duncan. Is that correct?'

After Charles had confirmed that he was, Eisenberg went on to say, 'I was in Rhodesia in the late 1970s, and met your father during the disastrous Bush War prior to Zimbabwe's independence. I was interested to hear that you are considering undertaking a fourth year of studies in Botswana and Namibia. As I know officials in these two countries quite well, I thought that I may be able to help you with some contacts?'

Charles was quite surprised that this apparent stranger already knew so much about him.

Eisenberg continued, 'As Sam mentioned when we first met, I am about to undertake a series of tutorials on Power and Governance, Political and Economic Organisation, and Understanding Behaviour, which I know your faculty is directly involved with. I have spent more than three decades in Her Majesty's Diplomatic Corps so have had considerable experience in a good cross-section of such relevant subjects, which could be of interest to you.'

'Yes indeed, I would definitely be interested in attending if I can. We are fortunate to have the benefit of your experience.'

'With the contacts that I have within the Diplomatic Corps in both of these countries and having met your father all those years ago, I would be delighted to be of some help. Perhaps you would like to take tea with me so that I can hear more about your proposed field studies?'

Charles had always possessed a disposition of considerable curiosity, but also one of reserve. As he had already started to warm towards this distinguished and charismatic ex-diplomat, he was quick to accept Eisenberg's invitation, and they agreed to meet at 3.30 on the following afternoon at Chapters of Durham tea rooms.

Prior to the meeting, Charles phoned his father at the Duncan family's ancestral home of Hartlington Hall, in the Dales of North Yorkshire.

'Father, yesterday, I bumped into a Philip Eisenberg, whom I had recently been introduced to by my tutor, Sam Prior. Eisenberg has joined the university as an Honorary Visiting Research Fellow. He told me that he had met you on various occasions in Rhodesia in the late 1970s and due to this connection he has offered to provide me with some introductions, should I be going on to Botswana and Namibia. Do you remember him?'

There was a moment of silence at the other end of the line, prior to his father's response.

'Charles, while I was in Rhodesia during those most troublesome times, I met a great number of people from many diverse backgrounds, including some visiting British diplomats at the home of a Second World War friend of your grandfather's. And if you say that this Philip Eisenberg was a member of the Diplomatic Corps, I did in all probability encounter him, although I shall have to check in my diaries to see when and where we did meet each other. I'll call you tomorrow, before you meet him.'

Dr Mathew Duncan had never told Charles much about the people he met during his time in Rhodesia. Or about the kidnap he had experienced by operatives of the Zimbabwe African National Liberation Army (ZANLA), or how he had been taken over the border to Mozambique, prior to his dramatic rescue by members of Rhodesia's security force. However, he had shared more light-hearted stories about various aspects of his primate behavioural studies, and how he had first met and fallen in love with his mother, Jan, a South African-born Rhodesian.

That evening, searching through his diaries, Mathew Duncan found a reference to having first met Philip Eisenberg, who had been staying in 1976 at the home of his father's war-time friend, Sir Colin Willock. In 1977 he had met Eisenberg a second time, when he had sat next to him at a dinner at the South African Embassy in Salisbury. On that occasion, he had written that Eisenberg had been a most engaging and agreeable person to spend the evening with. He had also noted how the young diplomat, of a similar age to himself, had shown considerable interest in his primate field studies on Rhodesia's border with Mozambique and, in particular, had been keen to learn as much as possible about the attitudes of the local people, both African and European, to Ian Smith's regime and the country's escalating Bush War.

*

The following day, Mathew called Charles to confirm that he had indeed met Philip Eisenberg all those years ago and had enjoyed his company. 'Do give Eisenberg my best wishes and tell him that it was good to hear from him again – and what a coincidence that he's ended up at Durham.'

His father's confirmation of their acquaintance led to Charles feeling more at ease about the meeting, and their rendezvous that afternoon proved to be a most informative and enjoyable occasion. After Charles had conveyed his father's goodwill message to his host, Eisenberg wasted little time before bringing up the subject matter that he had referred to on the previous day.

'Charles, prior to my retirement, I was attached to the British Embassy in the Democratic Republic of the Congo, and during this time the Chinese scramble for mineral resources in Africa had started to escalate. I was there when a major Chinese mining company completed a half-billion US dollar deal with a Congolese outfit, to develop and control some of the largest copper reserves in the world.

'China is currently facing a rapid depletion of its national mineral resources, and its growing economy is becoming increasingly thirsty for sustainable supplies of minerals in order to accommodate the country's future requirements. During the last ten or so years Chinese investment in Africa has had a more than twenty-five-fold jump, and the country is gaining increased control over Southern Africa's mining industries. Beijing's push to control and possess more of the continent's mineral resources will not end any time soon. Also, Japan is currently increasing its number of economic cooperative projects with the Botswana government, and thereby exerting more influence with a view to arriving at future beneficial agreements to gain access to the country's vast wealth of mineral resources.'

After Eisenberg had poured himself another cup of tea and taken a bite out of one of the restaurant's specialities, their popular home-made brownies, he went on to tell Charles more about the UK government's considerable concern about the sizeable increase of Chinese/African deals and control over the continent's mineral wealth.

'Charles, I shall come straight to the point about why I have asked you to have tea with me this afternoon. Beijing is now increasingly focussing on its mineral acquisitions in Botswana and Namibia, and many of their dealings are not always made public. Although our British High Commissions in both Gaberone and Windhoek attempt to keep as close as possible an eye on China's sometimes clandestine activities, reports from people working in the field have frequently proved to be invaluable for our information. And that is where you could well help the FCO to do its job.'

After Eisenberg took a further sip of tea, he said, 'I should stress from the outset that such source data gathering from local people on our UK government's behalf by no means represents spying on them. But rather, while going about your usual daily research project, just listening to what people are saying. Especially if they have been speaking about having come across foreigners applying for mineral rights and making land acquisitions within their homelands. Such instances will in all probability be Chinese representing their country's major mining corporations. And Charles, all that you would be requested to do would be to – in an unofficial capacity, naturally – pass on any relevant information that you consider might be of interest to them via, of course, an appropriate middle-man.'

Eisenberg went on to inform Charles that Botswana was the global leader in diamond production by value and was in the top five producers of other gemstones. And how recently they had managed to persuade De Beers, the world's biggest diamond concern, to relocate its global trading operation from London to its sleepy capital of Gaberone. This would enable Botswana to retain a major income from their current mineral wealth, once their diamond mines began to be exhausted.

He explained how the China General Nuclear Power Corporation (CGNPC) were currently trying to persuade the government of Namibia to authorise their acquisition of one of the biggest uranium deposits in the world.

'So you can see from all this how China is becoming firmly established in Southern Africa. And this is becoming of increasing concern to the West, in particular to the South African and UK governments. The forms of mining deals that China prefers in Southern Africa are diverse and a considerable number of these China-Africa agreements are kept in confidence between the governments concerned. It is very much about these clandestine deals, and even incidences of corruption, that our staff in Botswana and Namibia are particularly interested to hear about.'

Once their tea-time meeting was over, Charles thanked the one-time acquaintance of his father's and said, 'It has certainly been fascinating, what you have told me about China's considerable influence in Southern Africa, and their objectives. I would of course be willing to help my country by providing an additional source of FCO's information-gathering in Botswana and Namibia. However, this would be on the condition that I could be completely confident that such activities would not in any way compromise, or jeopardise, my anthropological research investigations with the Herero tribe, in either of the countries concerned.'

After Eisenberg had adequately reassured Charles that his studies would be unaffected, the two of them amicably shook hands. An onlooker might have supposed they had just achieved a mutually satisfactory financial transaction. In parting they agreed to meet again in the near future, so that the ex-diplomat could provide Charles with introductions to the High Commissions in Botswana and Namibia.

*

It was at the Klute nightclub, the converted boathouse by the Elvet Bridge over the River Wear in Durham, that Charles first set eyes upon Christiane Lüneberg. Christiane had been sitting on a spacious leather sofa in the sophisticated surroundings of the downstairs bar, in the company of two girlfriends. It had been her rather guttural laugh that had first brought her to Charles's attention.

Charles had been on a Saturday-night pub crawl with two of his closest friends, prior to ending up in the chill-out atmosphere of this 'membership only' part of Klute; a membership seldom, if ever, open to freshmen, but usually only gained by extensive patronage of the club. It had been for this reason that Charles had established that the three most attractive girls sitting on the sofa opposite him, and obviously enjoying themselves, were in all probability second- or third-year students from the university.

It was perhaps Charles's apparent aloofness that gave people who didn't know him the impression that he suffered from a degree of shyness, especially whenever he was in the company of members of the fairer sex. But he had always been a person who once he had set his mind upon something, was determined to see it through.

As there had been something fascinating and beguiling about the girl with the guttural laugh, Charles, having during the course of the evening consumed more than his usual number of pints of Newcastle Brewery's strong 'brown ale', cast away any vestige of shyness. He led his two friends over to the three girls and introduced himself immediately to Christiane. And it did not take long, after they had bought the girls drinks, for them to accept the boys' invitation to accompany them to the top floor of the building.

It was in the dimly lit surroundings of this nightclub that the university students so frequently ended up on their Saturday nights. And if they had not already arrived with a partner to dance with, there was always the hope of meeting an attractive person to join them under the soft lights of the crowded dance floor. It was also well appreciated that dancing in such an intimate environment could often lead to a more romantic and tactile relationship with their partner.

For Charles, the evening had turned out to be a great success, with all six of them having enjoyed a great deal of laughter and talk of mutual interests, particularly with Charles having felt how much he had in common with his new friend. And when they parted in the early hours of the Sunday morning, Christiane agreed with Charles's suggestion that they should meet again and gave him the telephone number of the flat that she shared with her two friends.

Charles phoned Christiane on the following Wednesday, and they agreed to meet for a drink early on the Saturday evening at the Swan & Three Cygnets. Although Charles had been nervous about phoning her, and had half expected his invitation to be turned down, he was delighted how pleased she sounded to hear from him. Christiane later told him that after they had met at Klute, it was the first time she had given her telephone number so readily to a stranger and she wondered whether he would ever call, if they would see each other again.

Charles arrived at the hostelry well in advance of the time that they had agreed to meet and chose a small table by the window overlooking the river, which also had a commanding view of both of the inn's entrances. When Christiane arrived, he was bowled over by her beauty. After giving her a rather nervous kiss on both cheeks and venturing some initial somewhat stilted and embarrassed small talk, it didn't take long for them to relax in each other's company. To an outsider, it must have appeared that they had been intimate friends for some time.

Christiane began by saying, 'Charles, when we met at Klute the other evening, no doubt you recognised from my accent that I do not come from the United Kingdom? I'm German.' She went on to tell him that she was currently in her third year of a four-year BA degree course in Modern Languages and Cultures.

Charles was quick to respond. 'Christiane, I could not be more delighted to have met you, and to now have a German friend!' They both laughed, and Charles told her that he too was in his third year in his studies for a BA in Social Anthropology and was hoping to achieve a sufficiently good degree to study for a PhD in Southern Africa.

Christiane took another sip of her chilled Chilean Sauvignon and gave him the most wonderfully engaging smile that he could recall ever having seen. Her Teutonic deep blue eyes became ablaze with interest about his future plans and she said, 'It is difficult to believe in such a coincidence, for I could be in Namibia too in connection with my particular interests and research.' As they both became keen to hear more about their respective future plans and studies, and were enjoying each other's company so much, they decided to take a cab to the popular Hollathan's restaurant in Chester-le-Street to have dinner together.

During dinner, Christiane told Charles about her German ancestry, and the reason why she had decided to visit Namibia during her fourth year of degree studies.

'My great-grandfather, Duke Gustav von Braunschweig-Lüneberg, had served as a senior representative of the Ministry of Foreign Affairs in German South West Africa during the latter part of the nineteenth and early twentieth centuries. He had worked directly with the German politician Leo von Caprivi, who succeeded Otto von Bismarck as German Chancellor.

'Charles, you may be already aware that it was at this time that the German administration signed an agreement ceding the islands of Zanzibar to the British in exchange for Heligoland, an archipelago just north-west of Hamburg, as well as a two hundred and eighty-mile strip of the Bechuanaland Protectorate, no wider than twenty miles in places, sometimes referred to as the Okavango Panhandle.'

She laughed and said, 'Evidently my great-grandfather, who played a major part in this exchange, had been delighted about this latter acquisition, which he had aptly named the Caprivi Strip after the German Chancellor. He believed that as the eastern end of the strip ended up on the Zambezi River, this would provide his fatherland with a route from South West Africa to Germany's East African territories.' Christiane chuckled again. 'Of course, what he had not taken into consideration, or perhaps was not even aware of, was that the Victoria Falls and the rapids on the lower part of the Zambezi on the borders of the Rhodesia's and Mozambique were unnavigable, a factor that Dr David Livingstone had found to his detriment!

'At the beginning of the twentieth century, before General Lothar von Trotha became governor of the colony, my great-grandfather served as a senior colonial administrator under the previous governor, Theodor Leutwein. It is for this reason I wish to investigate whether my ancestor had any personal involvement in the atrocities that took place during this period of Germany's colonial rule of South West Africa.'

Charles was stunned: he found it hard to believe that this bewitching girl he had so recently met at Klute was intending to undergo a parallel course of research in Southern Africa. It seemed like a heaven-sent coincidence. Instinctively, he reached across the table to squeeze her hand affectionately. He had difficulty choosing his words. 'Christiane, I was delighted to meet you – now this amazing coincidence that our studies are going to take us to the same place, and the possibility that we could well meet up in Namibia is quite incredible. It is a rendezvous which has to happen!'

Charles had always been curious about the background of people he had become interested in and, in this case, he was fascinated by the German girl now sitting so close to him. For with her long brown hair, deep blue eyes and the coquettish tilt to her head, her whole disposition appeared to him to embrace all the attributes of a natural beauty. So, for the rest of the evening he couldn't help asking her as many questions as he could; to learn more about her ancestors, and how this could be relevant to his future studies on the Herero tribe, as well as about her current family and her upbringing in Germany.

Christiane had seemed rather embarrassed when she told him, 'I was christened Christiane Sophia von Braunschweig-Lüneberg – my family are descendants of the Duchy of Brunswick. The elder son is entitled to be referred to as the Duke of Braunschweig-Lüneberg. After my great-grandfather had served the Imperial German Government in Southern Africa, he always insisted on being known by his inherited title and full name as Duke Ferdinand Gustav von Braunschweig-Lüneberg. He had always liked to remind people of his noble lineage, that it derived from the German royal dynasty of Hanover. But don't worry, you can just call me Christiane Lüneberg!'

*

During the final months of their third year at Durham University, amidst the obligatory time they had to spend at tutorials with regards to their respective degree studies, they were frequently seen in each other's company. However, prior to Charles's departure for Botswana in the late autumn of the year, they had arranged to visit each other's homes, first in Germany and afterwards in England. Ostensibly, this was to discuss in more detail how the findings of their anthropological and cultural studies could possibly assist each other's projects. Although quite apart from their mutual attraction to one another, they had recognised how very important it was to try to get across to their respective parents how the opportunity of sharing such data could be of mutual benefit in their future studies.

One evening, shortly before Charles visited Christiane's family home, she was giving him an account of her rather aristocratic family history. 'I hope I am not boring you too much about my ancestry, Charles, but I thought that it was important for you to know as much as possible about my background, so that when you meet my family at Schloss Braunschweig you will not be too put off by the solemnity and formality of the place.

'During the Second World War my uncle, Augustus, the eldest son and thereby the heir to the dukedom, was killed during the Russian army's recapture of Stalingrad, so when my grandfather died my father, Günther, his second son, inherited the dukedom. However, he immediately relinquished the title, for not only could he ill afford to live up to the expectations of holding such a social position, but he preferred to retain the title that he had always been known by, Count Lüneberg of Schloss Braunschweig. Having done away with the Braunschweig part of our surname, since the mid-1950s our family have simply been known as the Lünebergs. Although it was before I was born, I could not agree more with my father's decision to forfeit his ancestral ducal trappings.'

2

SCEPTRED N'GAMILAND

Charles arrived at the British High Commission in Gaberone in November 2003, and was invited to have lunch with Colin Patterson, a contact given to him by Philip Eisenberg. After Charles gave his name through a small speaker to the left of the building's main entrance, above which the Union Flag fluttered graciously, the door was unlocked and he was greeted by a tall, glamorous African receptionist, who guided him to a small office on the second floor. A smart polished brass notice on the door recorded that it was the office of Mr Colin Patterson MBE, HM's Secretary for Economic Development.

Colin Patterson was a medium-sized man in his early forties with broad shoulders, close-curled blond hair, a military moustache and piercing blue eyes. If his firm handshake was anything to go by, Charles was aware that this was not a man to be trifled with. And, as he was being directed to a chair by the window, an assistant poured them both sizeable mugs of coffee, without asking, and left the room as hastily as she had arrived.

After a general preamble about how Charles's British Airways flight from London had been, Patterson didn't waste any time in getting down to the main reason for their meeting.

'You of course are not being asked to do anything at all clandestine, but rather while you are carrying out your anthropological studies on the Herero tribe in N'gamiland, if you were to hear about, or to see, any meetings between the Herero tribespeople and Chinese, or even Japanese, nationals we would very much like to be informed about these. In particular, if there were any incidences or even rumours that foreigners were trying to acquire mineral rights within the Herero's tribal lands.'

This was just what Charles had been expecting to hear after his initial briefing and he nodded his agreement. He waited for Patterson to continue.

'As you may be well aware, I have recently received through the embassy's diplomatic bag a comprehensive report from one of the Diplomatic Corps highly respected elders, Philip Eisenberg, whom I am told has already put you fully in the picture as to how the Chinese are slowly but surely making sizeable inroads in their push to control the continent's mineral wealth. Also, how some of their activities have resulted in clandestine commitments that have taken place between the Chinese and local tribal chiefs, which in some cases have involved both bribery and corruption.'

After Patterson had taken another sip of his coffee, as he stared directly at Charles through his deep-set eyes, he said, 'When you arrive at Maun I have arranged for you to be met by an African colleague of ours, by the name of Mothinsi, who is himself a Herero, and who will drive you to a small lodge to the south-east of the old wooden Maun bridge overlooking the Thamalakane river. Here, in the seclusion of the lodge, he will tell you everything that he knows about the increased incursions of Chinese to this region of Botswana, and about various rumours of their suspicious dealings with elders of the governing Batauana tribe.'

'What happens if I do hear anything that I believe might be of interest to you?' Charles asked.

'Mothinsi is to be your main contact in N'Gamiland, and he will let you know the most convenient and safest way for you to pass on the type of information that we are after; in particular, with regard to Chinese nationals seeking permission to prospect or to acquire the sole mineral rights from the tribal landowners. However, he has a cousin, Tjipene, living in the same village that you are going to – in all probability he will be the one to whom you will be asked to pass on any relevant information. Mothinsi's cousin can also be totally trusted.'

'I see. I can't guarantee that I will hear of anything that will be of interest to your department, although I am course willing to help – providing, as I said to Mr Eisenberg, that it does not impact on my academic studies.'

'Of course, Mr Duncan, that is understood. Hopefully this will be a mutually beneficial arrangement, and the contacts we provide you with will be helpful in your interaction with the Herero tribespeople.'

With that, the meeting drew to a close and the conversation at the lunch that followed at the four-star Caravela Portuguese restaurant was about everything other than the activities of MI6 in Botswana. It focussed rather around the recent success of the British Lions in Rugby Union's Six Nations; how the heavy rains in the early spring in the north of England had affected the grouse populations on Charles's family estate among the Yorkshire moors; about mutual concerns with regards to the radical cuts that had been currently taking place within Britain's armed forces; and the ultimate ability of Great Britain to adequately be able to defend itself.

Just prior to Charles taking the taxi to the airport, Patterson told him how very much he had enjoyed their meeting, and how he only wished that they could have the opportunity to get together again but that this would be impossible. 'Regrettably, for security reasons, this is to be our first and only meeting, and it will be of the utmost importance for you not – under any circumstances – to attempt to contact me direct. Any intelligence-gathering you are able to do on our country's behalf must be confined to communications via Mothinsi, in Maun.'

As the taxi negotiated its way through a tangle of unruly traffic on the Queen's Road, and afterwards during the Air Botswana flight over the massive sandscape of the Kalahari Desert to Maun, Charles could not help but feel a little bit like an adventurous schoolboy, about to embark on a James Bond-like mission in deepest Africa.

*

Mothinsi's broad, charming smile well illustrated his welcome to Charles at Maun's small international airport, and he had immediately taken the larger of his two cases and thrown it into the back of his 1970 4x4 Dodge pickup. During the ten-kilometre drive down to the Thamalakane river, Mothinsi questioned Charles excitedly about his life in the UK, his time at university and whether he was married or was about to take a bride.

It had been over a cold Castle beer, while they were seated on a small veranda in front of the lodge, fanned by a refreshing breeze coming down the river, that he said to Charles, 'My grandfather was a white farmer, married to a Herero woman, and ten years after Bechuanaland Protectorate's independence from Great Britain in September 1966, I was employed as a junior driver by Riley's Transport. Riley's is a long-standing transport company in the region, which over many decades has been mainly responsible for the conveyance of goods from Francistown to Maun.

'In compliance with the Botswana government's policy of encouraging all previously white-owned businesses to have a good multi-racial representation on their boards, and due to me having been a long-standing employee of Riley's and a distant relative, through my grandmother, of Chief Tjamuaha, I have recently been appointed a member of the company's Board of Directors.'

Charles sipped the cold beer, finally relaxing after a long day's travelling and a brief interrogation about his personal life.

'So, you've lived in Maun since you were a child?' he asked.

'I've always lived here. When I was a young boy, Maun was just a small dusty village with no bank, clothes shop, hairdresser, bakery, barber or cinema, although there was a small strip of tarmac on the road between the District Commissioner's office and the small post office. The Riley's Hotel and hardware store represented the hub of village life, but for us youngsters we would often hitch a lift on the back of one of Riley's Bedford trucks as far as the old wooden bridge here, and swim from this small beach just in front of us.'

As the conversation moved on, Mothinsi told Charles that he had recently received an increased number of reports about how representatives of Chinese mining companies were coming to Botswana, and attempting to solicit mineral rights agreements with a number of the local tribes, which included the Batauana, Bayei, Herero and the Mambukushu.

'Charles, this concerns me greatly. In my opinion, some of the tribal authorities are being taken advantage of by being offered little compensation to enable foreigners to prospect for minerals on their tribal lands and, in some cases, selling their respective mineral wealth for little benefit to the rank and file of the tribes themselves. Also, I have recently become aware of an increased number of cases where some tribal elders, without knowledge of their chiefs, have received personal bribes, enabling Chinese corporations to prospect for minerals on tribal lands. And it could not be more regrettable that there are rumours that even some of the tribal elders from my Herero tribe are being tempted by such solicitations.'

Later on in the evening, after they had been served a tasty, well-seasoned buffalo steak, they sat around a smouldering campfire in front of the lodge, which had the benefit of the fire's copious smoke keeping the mosquitoes at bay. Mothinsi told Charles about how, some forty years ago, so much of the Okavango Delta region had been saved from the destruction of its wildlife heritage by big game-hunting safaris. And that it had been due to the opposition by the indigenous African tribes to such destruction that the Okavango Delta was now internationally recognised as representing one of Africa's Seven Natural Wonders.

It was at this stage of the evening that Charles told Mothinsi about his father's time in Africa during the 1970s, how his father had always been a dedicated naturalist and conservationist and had loved the time he had spent in Africa.

'My father first visited the continent when, as a graduate of primatology, he had studied the Grauer's eastern lowland gorilla in the Kahuzi-Biega National Park in Zaire, now the Democratic Republic of the Congo, as a part of his university's doctorate thesis. After being awarded his doctorate at Emory University at Atlanta in the United States, he had returned to Africa to study a number of other primate species in Southern Rhodesia, prior to Zimbabwe's independence in 1980. And only last week, when my father was seeing me off from our home, he told me how very much he had regretted not having taken the opportunity to visit Botswana, especially the Okavango Delta, a region that he had been told so much about.'

'Your father must indeed be a truly dedicated man. In my youth, the early 1960s, we used to visit a European couple called Robert and June Kay, a little further upstream from here. They were given permission by Mohumagadi Moremi, the Queen Regent of the Batauana, to establish a camp there. The Kays were fascinating people – they owned two pet lions, three cocker spaniels, a bull terrier, an assortment of poultry and an amphibious DUKW vehicle called "Shaka Zulu" after the warrior king of the Zulus. They always seemed pleased to see us;

they would tell us many interesting stories about their travels, and the different animals that they had encountered.

'It was Robert and June Kay who were undoubtedly responsible for me taking an interest in the future welfare of the wildlife in the delta, which in turn led to my support for the conservation measures that were to be adopted by the tribal elders. It had been after my initial meeting with the Kays that it later turned out that they were to be the two main Europeans behind the establishment of N'gamiland's Fauna Conservation Society. My father's relative, Jack Ramsden, was a founder member – quite ironic for as a young man, he had a reputation of being a fine shot, and was inclined to shoot at any beast that he clapped his eyes upon. Whether he needed the meat or not.'

Mothinsi told Charles about the background and the battle that had taken place between the tribal authorities and the colonial District Commissioner, and the subsequent establishment of wildlife sanctuaries in the delta.

'In the early 1960s, with Kenya and Tanganika, now Tanzania, gaining their independence from Great Britain, a number of East African safari firms were trying to lease substantial tracts of the Okavango Delta, in order to secure new territories for their big game-hunting safaris. And it was a policy that the British District Commissioner, Mr Eustace Clark, had been enthusiastically encouraging. It was pointed out that as far as he had been concerned, the revenue from the hunting parties would "help to finance the impoverished Protectorate", and at the same time save the British taxpayer money. That was before the discovery of Botswana's vast mineral resources. As for the animals, he said they could fend for themselves.'

He told Charles that the Kay's were alarmed about the possibility of seeing the delta's wildlife heritage being eroded in such a fashion. June Kay started writing numerous articles for national and international papers and magazines to highlight the danger to the long-term survival of the delta's wildlife. In particular, whether the East African big game-hunting safari firms should be allowed to continue to receive extensive hunting concessions throughout the Okavango Delta.

'Also, at this time her husband, Robert, did as much political networking as possible between the local inhabitants of Maun, both European and African, Batauana and Bayei, in his attempt to counter the District Commissioner's strategy of generating funds from the hunting safari operators, as opposed to looking at other potential income sources through wildlife tourism. And during such networking Robert, to the disgust of the DC, had held several meetings with the Queen Regent. These had been aimed at lobbying the newly created N'gamiland Fauna Conservation Society's objective for a significant area of seven hundred square miles to be set aside for a reserve, and for the new reserve to be named in honour of the Royal House of Moremi.'

Mothinsi explained that the DC had been so angered when he heard that there was to be a meeting of the Tribal Council, made up of elders and sub-chiefs, held under the Chairmanship of the Queen Regent to make a final decision, that he had told one of his colleagues (as reported in one of the Fauna Conservation Society's newsletters), 'The creation of a tribal game reserve is as impossible as the thirteenth moon.' Also, how some of his colleagues had been sceptical and were recorded as saying, 'Create an African-sponsored game reserve? Impossible. Try teaching them to grow rice in swamps instead. Teach an African, hunting people, to preserve the very animals of which they live... Not in this day and age!'

June Kay had published the DC's comment widely, and at the same time she had highlighted how virulently opposed he was to the establishment of a reserve by a tribal authority. This was in spite of the DC having been told that for the first time in many years the Batauana and Bayei had been able to agree on a common issue, and that their tribal feuds were now a thing of the past.

'The Queen Regent's son, Letsholathebe, the future Kgosi, who was studying in the UK, was at home on vacation at the time of the all-important 1962 Kegotha meeting,' Mothinsi said. 'Before he returned to the UK, the future king told his subjects, "In a few days I am leaving you with a priceless heritage of game animals in your care. On my return I expect to see that this heritage has been preserved."' Mothinsi proudly added how his uncle, Jack Ramsden, had addressed the Kegotha after an old man had said 'No' to the idea about a reserve, and that the Batauana and Bayei should not be in a hurry over this matter.

'I remember my uncle really struggled to conceal his irritation at this negativity. He said, "When our Chief Letsholathebe returns, shall he say to us, *I left you with much game, but where is it now?* And then will he ask you, *What have you done with all my game, you very old man? Is it due to you, because you stood in the path of those of my people who were ready to protect it?*"' Jack Ramsden's passionate response to those attending the Kegotha had evidently greatly helped to change the minds of those who had initially been against the establishment of the Moremi Reserve.

Charles was given an insight into how such new legislation can result in being adopted into the law of the land. Mothinsi explained how the Tribal Council was composed entirely of influential elders and sub-chiefs, who acted as a steering committee between the King or the Paramount Chief or their representatives on the one hand, and the tribesmen – the 'electorate' – on the other. Also, how in some cases it was the Council who actually had the power even to overrule the head of the tribal authorities themselves.

'Although Chief Tjamuaha represents an influential sub-chief in the Herero dynasty, his influence in the Tribal Council is minimal in comparison to that of the King of the Batauanas.'

Charles was fascinated by Mothinsi's account of how the Okavango Delta had become one of the world's most magical destinations for the viewing of endangered species. And to see how proud Mothinsi was that some forty years ago, one of his relatives had played such an important role in the establishment of the Moremi Wildlife Reserve, the first of such wildlife sanctuaries to be wholly African-sponsored, and how the Okavango Delta now represented Botswana's second most important income resource derived from wildlife tourism, with many of the world's most important game-viewing safari firms operating in the delta.

Charles had already read about how environmentally, the Okavango Delta was comprised of permanent marshlands and seasonally flooded plains, with a wetland system that is almost intact. Also, how it represents one of the very few ecosystems whose crystal-clear waters, which flowed from their source in the Angola highlands from the north-west of the delta, did not reach either a sea or an ocean. But rather were soaked up and disappeared into the vast sandscape of the Kalahari Desert.

After the orange flicker of the embers of the campfire were no longer emitting their protective smoke screen against the invasive mosquito, their conversation had ended just before midnight. But this had been just after Mothinsi had said, 'It is very much my hope that now, with more time available to me, I can continue with my support of the conservation of the Delta's wildlife heritage, and also undermine the corruption and exploitation by the foreign operators and national corporations trying to secure Botswana's mineral wealth. I shall do everything in my power to stop them, you have my word.'

*

The following morning, Charles was woken by the far-carrying call of an African fish eagle, often referred to as the 'Voice of Africa'. Mothinsi drove him back through the already quite sizeable township of Maun, on a six-hour journey to the north-west of Botswana. Three-quarters of the way to his destination of Nxau Nxau, Mothinsi had stopped at a small petrol station, where he had arranged to meet one of his cousins, Tjipene. Whilst the Dodge pickup was being refuelled, Tjipene immediately climbed into the vehicle.

'My cousin is to be the person that you must make contact with, should you hear any rumours about foreigners arranging to have clandestine meetings with members of the Herero tribe,' Mothinsi explained. 'Particularly if such rumours are connected with tribal elders, who could be tempted to accept bribes in return for enabling foreigners to prospect for minerals on tribal lands.'

Charles shook hands warmly with Tjipene.

'My cousin is a confidant and trusted advisor to Chief Tjamuaha and is usually present at the monthly meetings of tribal elders,' Mothinsi continued. 'And although on the surface of such meetings it appears that all the elders are loyal to Tjamuaha, the chief is aware that there are a few of his relatives who are jealous of his tribal power, who wish to benefit financially, and so are tempted to accept bribes from outsiders without the chief's authority. Due to the seriousness of these clandestine dealings, and the risks involved in passing on information to my cousin, it will be important for you to only approach him when you have something you consider to be of significance, and this should always be after Tjipene has been present at one of the monthly meetings. I suggest that if you could casually offer him a packet of cigarettes, you could conceal a note inside with the details.'

With the temperature hovering around 35°C and the dust from passing vehicles being wafted into the pickup around them, Charles went over to the small trading station behind the petrol and diesel pumps to purchase three cans of cold Castle. On his return, he toasted Mothinsi and Tjipene.

'It is my hope that my time with your tribe will be a successful and productive one. And should I learn of anything that I consider could prove to be in the long-term counter-productive to the welfare of your tribe, I shall do as you suggest and pass this on to Tjipene.'

After copious smiles and firm handshakes all around, Charles thanked Mothinsi for everything he had done for him and for telling him the story of the Moremi Reserve. Charles climbed down from the pickup and walked with Tjipene across the dusty tarmac road. They slid into his battered old grey Ford to continue the journey to Nxau Nxau in the north-west, via Gumare. At Nxau Nxau, Tjipene would introduce Charles to his tribal chief who had, through much correspondence, agreed to accommodate him in his village during his anthropological studies of Chief Tjamuaha's Herero heritage.

Nxau Nxau was some 125 kilometres from Gumare. At first, Tjipene drove along the tarmac road to Shakawe, on Botswana's border with Namibia, then he turned north onto a dirt road to Nxau Nxau, a journey that took just under four hours to complete. Tjipene told Charles that only four-wheel drive vehicles can negotiate the road during the rainy season, which luckily Charles had avoided.

As they drove along the hard-baked corrugated surface of the dirt track, Charles said, 'Tjipene, I am quite surprised that your vehicle will have any supportive springs left to boast about by the time we reach your village.' Charles had been bounced about the vehicle's cab to such a degree that it turned out to be the most uncomfortable journey that he had ever experienced.

However, during the drive Charles had been fascinated to see the many clusters of thatch-plumed mud-built dwellings, and the womenfolk in long, colourful dresses walking along the side of the dusty track with old oil cans filled with water balanced miraculously on top of their turbaned heads. Small groups of goats nibbled at everything within their reach, while ubiquitous poultry kept themselves occupied by pecking incessantly at the ground, narrowly missing being run over as Tjipene wrestled with the vehicle's wheel in order to avoid the sizeable pot-holes on the dirt road.

During the journey, Tjipene told Charles about the background of the tribal people inhabiting this north-western region of Botswana. 'The population is largely rural, heavily dependent on farming for their daily needs. The predominant ethnic groups are Batauana, Bayei, Bahereo, Bambukushu and the Basubiyn, with the smaller populations of the Banoka, Okavango's original inhabitants – the River Bushmen – the Bakgalagade, and the Herero. Most of these groups had their settlements along water courses, which they use for subsistence fishing and watering their livestock. They also plough the flood plains, growing maize and sorghum, with the Herero in the main being pastoral farmers. Not an easy life, but we must do all that we can to preserve it; we need the land to survive.'

Chief Moagi Tjamuaha, who was referred to by his people as 'Kgosi', lived in a small, whitewashed bungalow with a red-painted corrugated-iron roof, close to an assortment of thatch-plumed windowless *rondavels* (circular huts). As Tjipene's Ford pickup drew up in front of the chief's house, it was immediately surrounded by a pack of skinny, barking mongrel dogs, while a number of scantily dressed children gathered around the vehicle to see who had suddenly arrived within their midst. And as soon as Charles appeared, the children were all full of smiles pointing at his locks of blond hair. In those days, the village seldom had a white man visiting it.

Two enormous acacia trees stood like sentries on either side of the steps leading up to the small mosquito-netted veranda of the bungalow, and a boulder-strewn *kopje*, with scatterings of stands of yellow elephant grass, acting as an attractive backdrop to the small building. On hearing the barking of dogs, and the noises made by the children, the chief came down the steps of his bungalow to greet Tjipene, who quickly introduced him to Charles. Whilst taking tea on the veranda, Charles was delighted to note what a good command of the English language the chief had. It was a good opportunity to explain the main objectives of his anthropological studies.

After these initial formalities had been completed, Chief Tjamuaha told Charles that he would like him to attend the monthly meetings of his tribal elders, and that the next one was to take place at noon on the following Saturday. 'For this will provide me with the opportunity to introduce you to all those assembled and, in particular, for you to explain to them the reason for your presence, and for being an honoured guest in our village.'

The chief had summoned one of his assistants, Kisi, to take Charles and his luggage to the hut that had been set aside for him for the duration of his stay.

Kisi told Charles about the background of his new abode. It had been built in the mid-1950s to accommodate the occasional visit of one of the colonial District Officers who, on behalf of the British High Commissioner in Gaberone, and the District Commissioner in Maun, were responsible for the administration of tribal lands in the Bechuanaland Protectorate. It was built on stilts, in order to prevent the seasonal rains from flooding the floorboards; there was a small veranda, a stable door, a small four-paned window festooned with cobwebs, a table with a paraffin lamp on it, a couple of chairs and a wash-stand. In the middle of the room was a wooden double bed covered by a *kaross* (rug) made out of impala skins, which was raised just a few inches above the floorboards. And when Charles noticed the state of the soiled bed linen, he had been pleased that his mother had insisted that such items as a tropical sleeping bag, with a connected mosquito net, had to be included in his kit during his stay in such out-of-the-way environments.

A small cubicle to the rear of the hut provided a toilet facility, which had a wooden seat positioned over a deep hole in the ground. In the absence of a flushing system, there was a half-full bucket of cinders, and a small shovel to utilise in order to doss-down and cover the ablutions in the deep hole beneath. Just adjacent to this was a small door leading out to the rear of the dwelling. The hut had an overall covering of dust, with a faded zebra skin placed between the bed and the table. As both Charles and Kisi had also noticed that the floor had a generous scattering of rodent droppings over it, Kisi had been quick to tell a middle-aged woman, who had been standing by the door gaping at the presence of a European in their midst, to sweep up the droppings, remove the cobwebs from the small window and to make the hut as clean as possible.

During Charles's first evening in Nxau Nxau, Kisi had taken him to have something to eat in his small mud dwelling. Kisi told him how the Herero, like the majority of African people, pass on their tribal histories and traditions from generation to generation by word of mouth. Charles reflected that this was quite similar to the way wandering minstrels had told stories in mediaeval times in Europe.

'Until the middle of the nineteenth century there was no written language south of the equator,' explained Kisi. 'It was only then that the early missionaries, in their zeal to smash the old gods and replace them with theirs, introduced Africans to the *written word*. And with the increase of colonisation of Africa by the European nations, Africans in the east and the south had to learn of our past from the spoken sagas.'

After Kisi had guided Charles back to his hut, and had primed the lamp on the table, he said, 'After tomorrow's meeting of tribal elders, the chief is to introduce you to one of the wisest and most knowledgeable members of the Herero who live in this vicinity, from whom you will be sure to learn a great deal about our customs and traditions. Kgosi has asked me to bring you to tomorrow's meeting and to act as your go-between with him. Also, during your time with us, to provide you with any assistance that you may require.'

*

Charles's stay in the village was to begin with a potentially scandalous situation that he became completely unwittingly involved.

During the early hours of the morning, he had felt the *kaross* and the top of his unzipped sleeping bag, covering his naked body, being turned back. He first thought that he must be having some sort of sensuous dream about Christiane Lüneberg, with whom he had become infatuated. But before he could awaken to full consciousness, the next thing he experienced was the silky nude body of a young African lady placing her arms around him and drawing him close to her tightly formed breast.

Charles immediately struggled out of her grasp and the sleeping bag, flung back the *kaross*, and stumbled onto the floor. After gathering a towel around his waist he shouted, '*What the hell is going on here?*', whereupon the young woman, whose nude body was silhouetted by the beam of a full moon through the window, merely responded by beckoning him to return to her embrace, and on seeing that this handsome young European was about to leave her, just uttered a deep loud sigh of disappointment, and pulled the *kaross* over her nubile body to be left to sleep on her own. So, Charles retreated to the rear of the hut to gather up his clothes as quickly as possible and escaped through its back door to avoid a seemingly embarrassing situation.

On leaving the hut in the early hours of the morning, without a torch to guide him to Kisi's *rondavel* in the dark, it took Charles some time to recognise which one of the almost-identical mud dwellings was Kisi's abode. But as Charles had been stumbling around some of the huts it had not been long before he had been accompanied by a pack of mongrel dogs barking their protestations at having been disturbed in the early hours of the morning and, at the same time, in fear of a marauding leopard about to take one their pack. Fortunately, one of the villagers soon appeared from one of the *rondavels* to see what had caused the dogs to create such a commotion, to see whether a predator had come into the village to attack one of the dogs or was about to slaughter some of their valuable hens and geese. It was a spear-holding villager who guided Charles to the safety of Kisi's *rondavel*, where he had been welcomed and was able to sleep the night uninterrupted within the folds of a *kaross* of impala skins.

It had been some time later that Kisi had told Charles about some of the background of the previous occupants of the hut that he had had to vacate so swiftly, in the middle of the night. 'For some time it had been occupied by a variety of young ladies who were lending their bodies in return for a small cash payment, or for an equivalent valued gift. Although as far as the chief was concerned the girls were acting illegally, but in order not to conflict with the actions of some of his elders, he had decided to turn a blind eye to such a practice. However, more recently, due to outbreaks of both STIs and AIDS in the village, the tribal elders, some of whom had regularly taken advantage of the services that the teenage girls had provided, had agreed with Ngosi that such a facility should be now permanently closed.'

'Probably some of the girls saw that a handsome man had moved into the house alone and thought that she might see if you were interested. I'm sure she will leave you alone now you've made your feelings clear.' Charles hoped that it was indeed the only time he would be woken by an uninvited stranger climbing into his bed.

3

HUMBLING OF THE HERERO

It was under the tortuous branches of a huge baobab tree that Chief Tjamuaha held his monthly Saturday-morning meeting with his tribal elders. He started the meeting by saying, in a deep, booming voice, 'Mr Charles Duncan here is going to be a guest in our village for the next three to four months. He is an anthropologist and is keen to learn as much as possible about our tribal customs and traditions. And during his time with us he wants to see how our ways of living and lifestyle differ, if any, from those of our Herero tribal cousins who had remained in our original homelands of South West Africa. This was, of course, after our ancestors had fled from the German colonists to the Bechuanaland Protectorate, at the start of the last century.

'For, as all of you know, the Herero living in Namibia today are the descendants of those who had managed to escape the massacres carried out in 1904 by the German colonists in South West Africa. As our ancestors have informed us, the uprising of the Herero and Nama peoples occurred soon after the breaking of a treaty that they had signed with the Germans, due to the latter's policy of stealing our cattle and tribal homelands. Moreover, those of our Herero ancestors who had escaped from the German military onslaught, and who did not flee across the border to the safety of this, our adopted country, were either kept as agricultural slaves, or were incarcerated in concentration camps which their colonial masters had established.'

A murmur of discontent spread around the elders. Chief Tjamuaha held up his hand to signify quiet so that he could conclude his address.

'After Mr Duncan has been our guest here he intends to travel to Namibia to continue with his studies of our Herero tribe and he has particularly asked me to tell you that during his time with us he would like to be referred to by only his Christian name, Charles. And although he has been able to read a certain amount about the history of our tribe, he is keen to learn more about our customs and traditions. In particular, to hear about any tribal legends and stories with regards to the flight of our forefathers from our ancestral homelands in South West Africa, almost one hundred years ago.'

After Charles had thanked the chief for his kind welcome, and for informing the elders about the purpose of his stay with them, he got up from his stool and went around each of them to warmly shake their hands. Although the majority of the elders beamed welcoming smiles of obvious friendship, he could not help detecting from the facial expressions of two of the more portly of them, what seemed to be a degree of reserve and hostility.

Charles had found the chief's Saturday-morning monthly gathering of elders, and other invitees, to be an ideal opportunity for him to meet the senior members of this small part of the Herero tribe. And he had felt that it had been a good omen for having received so many smiles of welcome and obvious signs of friendship from the majority of those present. Although, he could not help feeling a little concerned about the two sullen-looking elders who had rejected his outstretched hand of friendship and had failed to make direct eye contact with him. But Charles considered that this could have been due to them not liking the idea of having a foreigner, a European, living for some time in their village.

In Charles's previous months of readings about the Herero tribe, he had found that the name actually referred to a group of tribes. The various tribes forming the Herero group all spoke a common Bantu language – the Himba (also known as the Ovahimba), Herero, Tijimba and Mbanderu.

During his research, he had noted that it had been during the seventeenth and eighteenth centuries that the Herero migrated to what is now Namibia from the east and had established themselves as herdsmen at the beginning of the nineteenth century. The Nama people who had migrated northwards to South West Africa were soon followed by white merchants and German missionaries. At first, the Nama began displacing the Herero, which had led to warfare between the two ethnic groups, a state that had persisted during the greater part of the nineteenth century. It was only later that the two peoples entered into a period of cultural exchange.

By the time of Charles's visit to Africa just over 100,000 Herero lived in Namibia, Southern Angola and Botswana. These populations were divided into two groups: the one that entered the Gobabis area east of Windhoek and became known as the Mbanderu (or Eastern Herero). The other group, who had crossed the Kunene River and settled in the Kaokoveld in the rocky, dry north-western part of Namibia, was made up of the Tijimba and the Himba. Until the arrival of the European settlers, the Herero had been semi-nomadic pastoralists.

In the late nineteenth and early twentieth centuries, imperialism and colonialism in Africa was at its peak. European powers were hungry for trade routes and railways, as well as land. In 1842 some of the Herero chiefs had joined forces with the Namas and Orlams to organise a united resistance against other Herero chiefs over their respective lands and livestock. By the mid-nineteenth century more European explorers, traders and missionaries began to move into central and southern South West Africa. And in 1883 the German merchant Franz Adolf Eduard Lüderitz entered into a contract with the native elders, which one year later became the basis for German colonial rule.

At the 1884 Berlin Conference, this region of South West Africa was awarded to the German government, without any of the country's indigenous population having been represented. This was a pattern at the time, when great swathes of the African continent were being awarded to conflicting European powers. After the Berlin Conference the German colonists had been quick to establish their presence in South West Africa by creating individual 'Protected Areas' with the local tribal chiefs. A paramount chief, Chief Maharero, signed a treaty with the Germans, but without consulting the other Herero chiefs, for he considered that this would strengthen his power. In fact, it weakened his standing among his fellow chiefs, and this led to yet more colonists moving into Hereroland.

This migration resulted in conflict between the colonists and the Herero herdsmen about access to land and water, with this being exacerbated by legal discrimination against the native populations. As a consequence of such conflicts, Chief Maharero was forced to break the treaty, but the Germans by this time had firmly entrenched themselves in their new colony of German South West Africa.

However, as Chief Maharero found himself unable to resist both the Nama tribe and the colonists, he signed another treaty with the Germans shortly before his death in 1890. During the ensuing power struggle, the chief's son, Samuel, who was backed by the German administration, rose to power. This caused a deep rift within the Herero people, as the other chiefs would have preferred someone with fewer ties to the German colonists.

In 1892, the settlers increased their theft of both cattle and tribal land, which led to a short-lived alliance between the Herero and Nama tribes, and a new conflict with their colonial masters. But this was soon crushed by the German military.

In 1903, the Herero people learned that they were to be placed in reservations, in order to leave more room for the colonists to own land and prosper. In 1904, the Supreme Chief of the Herero, Samuel Maharero, defied the Germans and led his people into battle. He called for a united resistance of the South West African tribal communities, both Herero and Nama, against the German settlers. And with an army of some 7,000 warriors, they were able to use the element of surprise to secure key victories early on in the fighting, and regained control of much of central South West Africa. However, with the arrival of more experienced soldiers, the Germans started to flex their military muscle in fortifying the region, with some 19,000 of their troops being stationed in the country, of whom 3,000 saw combat.

On 3 May 1904, General Adrian Dietrich Lothar von Trotha was appointed as Governor of German South West Africa and Commander in Chief of its colonial forces. He was directed to crush the native Herero rebellion. The general arrived in the colony on 11 June 1904, when the war against the Herero had been raging for five months. Up to that time the German command had not had much success against the Herero guerrilla tactics, and had suffered losses, a situation that von Trotha was determined to end.

The general's military background had been ably suited to take on such a challenge to Imperial Germany. He had previously served in the Austro-Prussian War and in the Franco-Prussian War. In 1884, von Trotha had been appointed Commander of the colonial forces in German East Africa (now Tanzania), and was ruthlessly successful in suppressing uprisings of the native population in the Wahehe Rebellion. During this time he had been temporarily posted to Imperial China, as Brigade

Commander of the East Asia Expedition Corps. He had been actively involved in suppressing the Boxer rebellion.

In October 1904 von Trotha devised a new battle plan to end the Herero uprisings. At the Battle of Waterberg he issued orders to encircle the Herero on three sides, so that the only escape route was into the waterless 'thirst-lands' of the Omaheke Steppe, in the western Kalahari Desert. When the Herero fled into the desert, von Trotha ordered his troops to poison water holes, to erect guard posts along a 150-mile line, and to shoot on sight any Herero man, woman or child, who attempted to escape. And to make his strategy to the Herero people absolutely clear, on 2 October 1904 von Trotha issued the infamous *Vernichtungsbefehl* (Extermination Order).

This official German 'colonial government order' was posted on all government buildings, and distributed throughout the colony, as well as being presented to the troops at roll-call. The general's proclamation read:

> *I, the great general of the German soldiers, send this letter to the Hereros. The Hereros are German subjects no longer. They have killed, stolen, cut off the ears and other parts of the body of wounded soldiers, and now are too cowardly to want to fight any longer. I announce to the people that whoever hands me one of the chiefs shall receive 1,000 marks, 5,000 for Samuel Maharero. The Herero nation must now leave the country. If it refuses, I shall compel it to do so with the long tube (cannon). Any Herero found within the German frontier, with or without a gun or cattle, will be executed. I shall spare neither women nor children. I shall give the order to drive them away and fire on them. Such are my words to the Herero people.*

Once von Trotha had issued his Extermination Order, it became clear to the civil governor, Colonel Theodor Leutwein, that his own authority had evaporated and he was relieved of his post. Historians have since argued that von Trotha's *Vernichtung* of the Herero was not a German governmental edict, but rather represented a colonial governor's bombastic proclamation, in a general's attempt to exercise what would now be referred to as psychological warfare on all those who had risen up against their imposed colonial masters. And some time after the proclamation, von Trotha was described by the German authorities in Berlin as a 'bad statesman, inadequate as a war leader and, generally, an ignoble, egoistic and hard-hearted man'. In his defence, some recorded how the general 'must have been sorely provoked by the unpleasant things that the Herero did to their prisoners-of-war'.

As a result of the order to exterminate all Herero resisting the German colonists, it was estimated that during the uprising seventy-five to eighty per cent of the indigenous population perished, with survivors having been scattered all over the country. Nevertheless, a substantial number of Herero did manage to flee across the border to the Bechuanaland Protectorate (now Botswana), where they became subsistence farmers growing grain and rearing sheep, cattle and fowl. From 1904 to 1907 the colonists' onslaught against the Herero and Nama was the first time that German imperialism had resorted to methods of genocide. During this period, it was estimated that between 24,000 and 100,000 Herero people lost their lives, and about 10,000 Nama.

On 22 April 1905 von Trotha sent a message to the Nama, mentioning the fate of the Herero, suggesting they surrender. The Herero had suffered much greater losses during the fighting than the Nama, with approximately 10,000 Herero having died, and many of those remaining had either fled or had been confined to concentration camps. The Nama failed to respond to this missive.

The southern coastal town of Lüderitz, flanked by desert and ocean, was the site of the worst of the German prisons, with the Shark Island Concentration Camp being connected to the mainland by a small causeway. The camp was situated at the far end of the small, barren island where prisoners suffered devastating exposure to the strong winds that swept Lüderitz for most of the year. In December 1906, it was reported that only four months after their arrival at the camp, over 290 Nama people had died.

Charles had noted that in the same year as the *Vernichtungsbefehl*, on 24 November 1904 the German Chancellor, Bernhard von Bülow, had recommended to Kaiser Wilhelm II that von Trotha's Extermination Order should be counter-commanded by stating: 'The politics of total extermination was unchristian; what von Trotha proposed could not be carried through; the politics of extermination was commercially senseless; and the proclamation would damage the German reputation among civilised nations.' However, the Kaiser delayed by fourteen days the process of countermanded von Trotha's proclamation of extermination, insisting that the general was to remain as the colony's governor and commander-in-chief.

When frequent reports of von Trotha's policy to use utmost force with terrorism and even brutal extermination began to circulate back in the Fatherland, von Bülow had become increasingly embarrassed when budgetary requests for more support for the colonial forces were voted down. He thereby requested Kaiser Wilhelm II to relieve the general of his command. And on 19 November 1905 von Trotha returned to Germany and was later appointed as an infantry general. At this time, anticolonial forces in Germany were in the ascendancy, and they even had a majority in the Reichstag. But after Chancellor von Bülow had been shamed by the lack of support for his colonial policies he dissolved the government in December 1906 and went to the country to request a mandate to carry on with Germany's colonial mission. He subsequently won the election, thereby giving the colonial parties a powerful mandate.

In April 1907, von Trotha's successor, General von Estorff, the new German Commander, wrote in his report that an estimated eighty per cent of the prisoners sent to the Shark Island Concentration Camp never left the island. Approximately 1,700 of the prisoners had died; over 1,000 of these had been from the Nama tribe. And there were accusations that Herero women had been coerced into sex slavery as a means of survival. In later years, it was generally considered that it would be more accurate to describe Shark Island's notorious camp as a place of extermination, rather than just being a work and concentration camp.

It was during this time that a German anthropologist, Eugen Fischer, visited the concentration camps to conduct medical experiments on race, using Herero children, as well as mixed-race children of Herero women and German men. The main objective of his research was to prove the superiority of white Europeans over Africans. Other experiments made by a Dr Bofinger involved injecting Herero who had been suffering from scurvy with various substances, including arsenic and opium, and afterwards researching the subsequent effects of these substances by performing autopsies.

It was estimated that up to 3,000 skulls were sent to Germany for experimentation. Eugen Fischer later became Chancellor of the University of Berlin, where he taught medicine to Nazi physicians. One of his prominent students was Josef Mengele, the doctor who performed genetic experiments on Jewish children at the Auschwitz concentration camp during the Second World War.

After the closure of the concentration camps, the few surviving Herero and Nama were distributed as labourers for the settlers of the German colony. And from that time all of the indigenous people over the age of seven were forced to wear a metal disc with their labour registration number and were barred from owning land and cattle.

In 1912, the colonists erected a memorial in the coastal town of Swakopmund, to not only celebrate the German victory, but also to remember the fallen Germans, for during the uprising over 700 soldiers were killed or went missing, and a similar number died from disease. It should be said that there was no mention on the monument of the great losses suffered by South West Africa's indigenous people.

In 1933, the Nazi authorities named a street in Munich after von Trotha. But in 2006 the Munich city council officially decided to change the name to Herero Strasse in honour of the victims of the war.

In addition to Charles having read much about the atrocious way the German colonists had dealt with the indigenous tribes of South West Africa at the beginning of the twentieth century, he decided that it would be relevant to his studies on the atrocities that the Herero and Nama tribes had been subjected to by the German colonists, to carry out some research on the ways that other European and Asian powers had treated the local inhabitants during their early days of colonial conquest. And he had found that the Germans were by no means the only colonists to have acted so cruelly towards their subjects, to mention only a few: the Dutch in the East Indies, the Japanese in China and Korea, the Americans in the Philippines, all had used the machine gun, the whip and forced labour to bring their subjects to heel.

He had found that the general European attitude had been eloquently expressed in the Report of the Commissioners into the Administration of the Congo State. For in 1904, under intense international pressure, King Leopold had appointed a three-member commission to investigate the allegations that the Belgians had used methods 'repugnant to civilised men' in ruling the then Congo Free State.

After the Commission had catalogued repeated instances of the shocking mistreatment of the native population, they came to what now seems a remarkable conclusion:

Although such conduct was not exemplary, in the ruling of 'inferior races', forced labour was 'absolutely necessary', in order to bring the natives along the road to civilisation ... In a word, it is by this basis alone that the Congo can enter into the pathway of modern civilisation, and the population be reclaimed from its natural state of barbarism.

It struck Charles that, less than sixty years later, after the Belgian government had given its colonial possession its independence in 1960, how many atrocities continued to be carried out by the inter-tribal political forces of President Tshombe and Patrice Lumumba, as well as by some of the European mercenaries financed by one side or the other.

Perhaps the worst atrocity in modern times that Charles had read about, in comparison to the massacre by the German colonists of the Herero and Nama people in South West Africa, was committed by Japan. This had been prior to the multiplicity of atrocities committed by the Japanese Imperial Army in Asia, during the Second World War. The Nanjing (Nanking) Massacre, or the Rape of Nanjing, took place during the Second Sino-Japanese War in 1937. This was after the Japanese had captured Nanjing, the then capital of the Republic of China. And during this period the army had murdered Chinese civilians, disarmed combatants, and perpetuated widespread rape and looting.

The International Military Tribunal for the Far East, held in Tokyo in 1946, estimated that over 20,000 Chinese were killed during the Nanjing Massacre. Although in 1947 China's official estimate put the figure dead, based on the evaluation arrived at by the Nanjing War Crimes Tribunal, as more than 300,000, all of whom were reported to have been slaughtered within a six-week period. The tribunal also estimated that over 20,000 Chinese women had been raped by the soldiers.

Charles had also been horrified to read how the French in Madagascar, in Equatorial Africa and in Indo China had suppressed uprisings with methods that, if lacking the heavy-handedness of the Germans, were not much less cruel. For in 1830, when the French had invaded and taken Algeria from the Ottoman Empire, it had been a brutal conquest. In 1843, a senior officer in the French expeditionary force in Algeria had written a letter to a friend later published by his nephew, which read: 'We must make war against the Arabs. In one word, annihilate all who will not crawl beneath our feet like dogs.' By 1845, the French military were reported to routinely put such annihilation programmes into practice. As an example, a General Aimable Pélissier, who was to become Marshall of France, reported the massacre of 1,500 people of the Berber tribe, who had taken refuge in a cave: *All in the name of civilisation.*

In the history of North America, Charles had noted that there had been over forty major conflicts between native Indians, European settlers and the army of the United States. And during this time, the US government recorded the loss of about 19,000 white men, women and children, and the deaths of over 30,000 Indians, although it was recognised that the number of Indians killed, and wounded, must have been very much higher than was reported.

Charles also found that the accounts which he read on the conflicts between settlers and indigenous populations were usually very one-sided, for they had been written by Europeans. In the United States, it was not until after 1970 that younger historians started to highlight the Indian point of view about their wars with the settlers. In particular, with the authors describing more fully the US government's failures and emphasising the impact of the wars on the native people and their cultures. For after the American Civil War, all of the Indian tribes were assigned to reservations, and the role of the US army was to keep them there.

The British too, judging by some accounts, had shown themselves to be ruthless in times of conflict. The Second Boer War

(1899–1902) had started under the pretence of Britain wishing to protect the rights of foreigners working in the gold fields of the Transvaal. But, in reality, it was Britain's wish to get her hands on the mineral wealth of the Afrikaner-controlled gold mines. For when the British forces, under the commands of Generals Kitchener, Milner and Roberts, had failed to get the better of the Boers of Dutch ancestry, they had plundered and destroyed the burghers' homesteads and farms. And then had pretended to act 'humanely by caring for the families of the fighting Boers', by transporting their women and children in cattle trucks to what they termed as refugee camps. But in fact, it was subsequently recorded that during the course of the Second Boer War the British were responsible for about 27,000 deaths of innocent women and children. They had been rounded up and placed in tented prisoner-of-war camps, with overcrowded unhygienic conditions, poor rations and almost no access to healthcare.

After reading about such historical events of massacres and atrocities, Charles was reminded what his father had told him about the events that had taken place during Rhodesia's Bush War, in which he had become indirectly involved during the 1970s. And after Zimbabwe's independence in 1980, how in December 1982 Robert Mugabe's ZANU/PF North Korean 5th Brigade trained forces had resolved what was termed as the 'Ndebele' problem, which resulted in the deaths of 20,000–25,000 tribal people in rural Matabeleland.

Also, that during his lifetime, how in 1994 the 100 days of slaughter of 800,000 people, mostly Tutsis by ethnic Hutus extremists, had taken place in Rwanda. And today, how the relationship between the two largest religions in the world, Christianity and Islam, were currently causing such high levels of religious hatred and hostilities, as was taking place in the Middle East and North Africa.

Charles had been pleased to read that the religious beliefs and practices of the Herero people, although still keeping the 'Holy

Fire', which symbolises the gift of life linking them with their ancestors. And that the majority of the Herero have converted to Christianity, which has resulted in the relationships between the tribal people in Botswana and Namibia being at peace with one another.

Charles wondered if mankind would ever learn from the multitude of mistakes that they had historically already made? But rather gloomily concluded that from the current state of so many nations' relationships with each other, what a sad reflection on *homo sapiens* it was that nationalism, and subsequent degrees of extremism, was returning into tribalism. Also, as was the case with General von Trotha's 'Proclamation of Extermination' of the Herero tribe, that those who have wished to inflict dominance upon others more often than not consider that they belong to a superior race or tribe to the one that they wish to destroy.

The 1985 United Nations Whitaker Report on Genocide recorded that the population of Herero between 1904 and 1907 had been reduced from 80,000 to 15,000. Such figures indicate that some 38,000 more Africans died in German South West Africa than the estimated 27,000 European Boers who had died, mainly from disease, in camps in South Africa, only a few years previously. However, the Whitaker Report was to classify the attempted extermination of the Herero and Nama as the first case of genocide in the twentieth century. It has since been argued by historians that the Herero genocide set a precedent in Imperial Germany to be later followed by Nazi Germany's establishment of the Holocaust death camps. However, Charles had noted that historians had convincingly argued that whereas Jewish suppression and elimination was an essential part of Nazi government policy, von Trotha's *Vernichtung* of the Herero, which palpably came from one man, should be seen in a strictly Prussian military context.

After Namibia's independence in 1990, many Herero living in Botswana expressed a desire to return to their roots. Although both governments were happy for such a repatriation to take place, any Herero leaving Botswana were obliged to leave behind their cattle and other possessions. By the turn of the twentieth century, an estimated 107,000 Herero were living in Namibia, South Angola and Botswana.

Lothar von Trotha had belonged to a prominent Saxon noble family and had been married twice, but his two sons died without descendants. The general's first wife, Bertha Neumann, died in 1905, but seven years later, at the age of sixty-four, he married the thirty-one-year-old Lucy Goldstein Brinckmann, who was Jewish and the daughter of a Frankfurt banker, in London. The general died of typhoid fever on 31 March 1920 at the age of seventy-one, whereas his much younger second wife died after the Second World War in 1958, at the age of seventy-seven.

While Charles was carrying out his research into the von Trotha family, he found it quite ironic that whereas in 1904 the German general had issued his *Vernichtungsbefehl* of the Herero, just under thirty years later, his successors in Adolf Hitler's Nazi Germany, had proclaimed that Jews were *Untermenschen* (sub-human). In 1935 many Jews lost their rights to be German citizens and, as a consequence, appalling numbers of them were gassed in the Nazis' concentration camps during the Holocaust.

However, it is unclear what happened in the Second World War to von Trotha's Jewish second wife, Lucy, *née* Goldstein Brinckmann, during the Nazi regime's early 1940s attempt to exterminate the Jewish race. Although she was reported to have prepared a war diary for publication, in order to 'weaken the accusations from abroad that the Germans in South West Africa had waged war against the black race so mercilessly and, in order to serve the truth'. But the diary, with its ample annexes and attachments, was never published, and its whereabouts are currently unknown. Charles had also been intrigued to learn that the original document of von Trotha's famous 'Proclamation of Extermination' had also mysteriously disappeared.

In 1915, during the Second World War, the League of Nations mandated German South West Africa to Britain's Union of South Africa. Although in 1966 the mandate was abolished by the UN, the Pretoria Government continued to rule the country, despite it being illegal under international law, until the country gained its independence as the Republic of Namibia in 1990.

4

GEMSTONE SKULDUGGERY

After Botswana and Namibia had gained their independence, the governments of China and Japan started to focus their attentions on both countries. Their international cooperative trading companies offered major support for infrastructure development, including housing, roads, railways, mining equipment and the provision of general expertise, in exchange for gaining processing rights and access to both country's vast mineral resources. And many Chinese and Japanese nationals were now operating in both countries.

Zhang Jinchu had completed a four-year bachelor's degree course at the Chinese University of Mining and Technology (CUMT), in the historic city of Xuzhou in China's Jangsu Province. And with a good knowledge of the English language, which Zhang had learnt in Hong Kong, he had managed to become an employee of the global multinational commodity trading and mining company Bazhong Hangheng Plc, and to operate in Botswana.

With China facing a rapid depletion of its own local mineral resources, and in order to overcome future shortages of essential mineral commodities, the government of China had empowered and encouraged a number of domestic state-owned and private companies to actively pursue mining deals throughout the world. With Africa having become the most desirable region for China- and Hong Kong-based companies to hunt for mining deals, Botswana being a global leader in diamond production by value, and in the top five producers of gemstones, Chinese and Japanese companies were increasingly vying with each other to secure the most profitable mineral mines which, more often than not, they preferred to own outright, rather than be in partnership with local companies.

Zhang's father, Li Yang Jinchu, had previously been a senior executive of the Zijin Mining Group, the operator of one of the world's biggest under-developed high-grade copper deposits at Kamoa, in the Democratic Republic of Congo (DRC). But in the late 1990s he had been headhunted by the Sanchuan Huanton Corporation International (SHCI), a unit of the Chinese state-owned Sanchuan Resources, one of China's biggest gemstone operators and a major copper producer. As SHCI was backed by the Chinese government, it had almost endless finance available to it, and the company already operated two mines in the Central African Copperbelt, the Ruashi copper and cobalt mine in the Congo, and the Chibuluma copper mine in Zambia.

However, Li Yang's company now had its eyes on Botswana's mineral wealth, particularly due to the rumours they had recently received about sizeable copper deposits being found in the Kalahari, as well as Botswana welcoming both Chinese and Japanese expertise in technology and manufacture, and because of the country's strong governance. This was the time that Sanchuan Huanton Corporation International was trying to compete with Li Yang's son's company, Bazhong Hangheng Plc, recognised to be the world's largest commodities trading company, which was also negotiating with the government to secure as many of Botswana and Namibia's mineral exploration rights as possible.

However, in spite of Sanchuan Huanton Corporation having recently been accused of illegal dealings with rogue states, having a history of busting UN embargoes to profit from corrupt despotic regimes, in particular having paid illegal 'kickbacks' to obtain oil in the course of UN oil for food programmes in Iraq, they had still been welcomed to operate by some countries in central and Southern Africa. But as Bazhong Hangheng Plc had endless resources and technical know-how, the company had currently a head-start on Li Yang's international corporation. For BH Plc had offered to provide Botswana with soft loans for infrastructure projects, involving the renovation of its railway network, low-cost housing, land survey and planning, road construction, health facilities, and agricultural technology.

Li Yang Jinchu had always encouraged his only son to embark on a career in mining, for he well recognised the significant financial rewards that could be derived from successful prospecting for minerals, and the potential of making clandestine closed-door deals. He knew that with some cunning, such deals could often be of benefit to not only the employers, but also to the potential of greatly adding to his own coffers. And now that his son had gained employment with Bazhong Hangheng Plc, Yang Jinchu saw that Zhang could become an important conduit of valuable information about other mining operatives during the course of his work in Botswana. For members of the Jinchu family were always open to potential illicit financial rewards, no matter whom or what company they were defrauding. The only crime that they recognised was for such corrupt dealings to be exposed.

Zhang had arrived in Botswana at much the same time as Charles. He had flown on a South African Airways flight to Johannesburg from Hong Kong, and then on to Gaberone, via Windhoek, the capital of Namibia, where he had spent ten days with some of the Bazhong Hangheng Plc senior management. He was made fully aware that the company expected him to negotiate mineral prospecting rights from the local tribal authorities, and to always keep them fully informed about any other Chinese or Japanese mining companies looking for minerals in the area that he was being sent to operate in. From Gaberone, Zhang had taken the Air Botswana flight to Gumare, where he had been met by a member of the Bayei tribe and taken to the Ramorwa Guest Lodge, where it had been arranged for him to be billeted.

Soon after Zhang's arrival in Gumare he had made contact with his father, who currently had his headquarters in Kitwe, on Zambia's Copperbelt. He had been anxious to let his father know about his conversations with Bazhong Hangheng executives in Gaberone, and exactly what they expected of him now that he was about to be one of their operators in north-western Botswana.

*

Two days after Chief Tjamuaha's Saturday monthly morning meeting, Kisi had taken Charles to meet Thopelo Riruako, the tribal elder who was reputed to be the most knowledgeable about the Herero's history and customs. Over a steaming mug of coffee, Thopelo reminded Charles about the flight of many of the indigenous population from South West Africa, after the German massacre of an estimated 65,000 of the Herero and Nama tribe, which had taken place during their rebellion against their colonial masters at the beginning of the twentieth century.

'My grandfather, with my great-uncle, were among those of us Herero who, after being surrounded on almost all sides by General von Trotha's soldiers, had managed to take the only route of escape available to them into the arid desert. It was only after my ancestor's arduous journey across the "thirst-lands" of the Kalahari Desert that they gained sanctuary in the Bechuanaland Protectorate, and were accepted by the local tribes, as well as by the then colonial administrators of Great Britain.'

As Thopelo had continued to speak about the Herero tribe, Charles had found it particularly fascinating when he said, 'In contrast to you Europeans, our tribe has a bilateral descent system whereby a person traces their heritage through their father's lineage, as well as by their mother's. Therefore, tribal hierarchy divides responsibilities for inheritance between matrilineal and patrilineal lines of descent.' Thopelo also told Charles that the Herero language, *Otjiherero*, a Bantu language, represents the main unifying link among the Herero peoples in Botswana, Namibia and Angola.

When Kisi began to suggest that it was time for them to leave, Charles said, 'I do appreciate you taking the time to talk to me Mr Riruako, I have a great deal I would like to learn and your help has been invaluable. I do hope we meet again soon.' The two men exchanged a warm handshake and agreed they would arrange another meeting in the near future.

*

Charles first encountered Zhang Jinchu in the bar of the Makgovango Luxury Inn in Gumare. He had heard Zhang telling the barman that he had only recently arrived in Botswana from Hong Kong, and that he was keen to meet and to get to know the local people as much as possible. Charles was quick to introduce himself and told Zhang that he too had only recently arrived in Botswana and was living in Nxau Nxau, over 120 kilometres to the north-west of Gumare. So, over a couple of Castle lagers, it did not take the two of them long to tell each other their main reasons for coming to Botswana. After sharing a buffet together in the Inn's restaurant, they exchanged their respective contact numbers, with Zhang saying, 'I would very much like to meet you again and to visit your village, as well as to talk to the tribal chief that you have spoken so much about.'

A fortnight later whilst he sat on a bar stool at the Makgovango Inn, Charles become conscious of two African men sitting in a more secluded corner of the bar, deep in conversation but repeatedly glancing at him. When he left the bar to go into the restaurant, Charles deliberately walked as near as possible to where they were sitting as he sensed something familiar about them. He recognised that they were the two surly-looking elders who had refused to shake his hand at the end of the chief's introductory meeting, a little more than a month ago.

During his meal that evening, Charles could only contemplate the reasons why the two men, who had obviously recognised him, had not come up to the bar and engaged him in conversation. After dinner he had returned to the bar, but the two Africans had departed.

*

Charles undertook his data-gathering sessions about the Herero tribe with Thopelo Riruako on a regular basis, and he found him to be most friendly and a mine of information about the history and customs of his tribe; a person to be trusted.

'Cattle,' Thopelo told him, 'are the most valued domestic animals in the Herero culture, and whereas cattle-herding and trading activities are only conducted by males, the women are responsible for milking, carrying out household chores, harvesting small field crops and taking care of their young children. Although the men are responsible for the cattle-trading activities, the women do most of the bartering for other goods. A dairy delicacy that you must try is a delicious sour milk called *omaere*, which the women are responsible for preparing. Goats and sheep are also used for meat consumption, and the goat milk is used to make dairy products, whereas goat skins are frequently used to carry babies on women's backs. And in Herero culture, goat dung is used for medicinal purposes.'

It was obvious to Charles that Thopelo was enjoying having a visitor who showed so much interest in the history and customs of his tribe, enquiring whether some of the Herero customs were gradually changing and adapting to the influences of the outside world. He was enthusiastic about answering the many searching questions, while Charles took copious notes about whatever he had told him.

It had been soon after one of these data-gathering sessions that on returning to his hut, Charles had found an envelope placed on the top of his sleeping bag with a poorly handwritten note inside. Attached to it was a badly focussed photograph.

The note read:

You will see from the attached image that soon after your arrival in our village, you took advantage of our honourable Chief's hospitality and bedded one of the village's maidens.

To Charles's horror, he was able to just detect in the photograph the image of his naked self, standing by his bed, which also showed an equally undressed African girl, with her arms outstretched as if enticing him to return to her embrace.

The unsigned note had ended:

In order to avoid a copy of the photograph finding its way to the presence of Chief Tjamuaha, we expect you to provide US $500.00, and for this amount to be left in your bathroom waste bin after your next visit to Gumare. And, as a warning, failing to leave the money as requested within the next three weeks, or any effort on your part to detect the source of this note, would immediately result in a copy of the photograph being passed on to our most respected chief.

Charles found himself in a state of considerable shock, and with the added dilemma as to what the best response should be. He needed to avoid at any cost a major embarrassment on his part, which could lead to him having to leave Nxau Nxau forever, and for his research work on the Herero tribe being seriously impeded. His next trip to Gumare was to be in five days' time, so at least it gave him time to consider what the best course of action should be. As Kisi had been the only person to have been told about how the young lady had so unexpectedly joined him in bed in the middle of the night, after he had fled his hut to the sanctuary of Kisi's *rondavel*, he decided in the first instance to discuss this attempt at blackmail with him. For this, after all, was very much based on circumstantial, as opposed to factual, evidence of him having seduced a young village girl.

Prior to going to Durham University, Charles had been educated at Wellington College in Berkshire and he had been told by his elderly grandfather, Sir Colin Duncan, 2nd Bt MC, that he had decided to send his father and Uncle Sebastian to Wellington for the main reason that he had been most impressed by the calibre of a number of Old Wellingtonians he had served as an officer in the 12th Royal Lancers, during the Second World War. Also, as the Duke of Wellington had served as a young subaltern in the 12th Lancers at the turn of the nineteenth century, he considered that it was appropriate for his sons to have the benefit of a well-rounded education at a school from which the old boys had served their country with such gallantry in both the First and Second World Wars. Wellington College had been built as a national monument to the Duke of Wellington and had been opened by Queen Victoria in 1859. On reflecting on his school days, Charles was reminded how the importance of being able to think and cope independently had constantly been drummed into them, and to remember the literary strength of the school's motto: 'Fortune Favours the Brave'. So, the following day, after having experienced an almost sleepless night worrying about the catastrophe that appeared to him to be almost unavoidable, he arranged to meet Kisi in his *rondavel*.

Kisi read the note and looked at the faded image of the naked girl with her outstretched arms, and the back view of a similarly naked Charles, and paused for quite a while before responding to what he had read and seen. 'My first reaction is to say how angry this makes me feel that you, as an honoured guest of our village, have been treated in such a way, and that an image of such a compromising scene in your hut should have been made. And I am truly appalled, but I must be given some time to consider what the best course of action is for you to take. Although my instinct tells me that you must not give the blackmailer or blackmailers the dollars that they are seeking, otherwise it could well develop into a regular demand.'

So, when Charles spent his next day and a half in Gumare, he decided to take Kisi's advice not to go to his bank to withdraw the amount of US dollars that had been demanded from him. Although on such occasions he always visited various trading stores to purchase sufficient supplies to cover his next two weeks at Nxau Nxau, collect any mail that may have arrived for him in a numbered PO box at the local post office and airmail a batch of letters to his parents, brother and a number of friends, especially to Christiane Lüneberg. He knew she would be currently staying at her parents' stately home at Schloss Braunschweig in Lower Saxony. He also took the opportunity to organise a long-distance call that evening, in the hope that she would be at home to receive it.

*

Prior to Charles coming out to Botswana, he and Christiane had visited their respective homes and met each other's parents. And although during their last summer term at Durham University they had become increasingly fond of one another, they had agreed that it would be prudent when in the company of their parents to act as if they were just friends. This was mainly to stress that the chief reason for them wishing to be together was their common academic interest in anthropology and social sciences. In particular, how sharing some aspects of their forthcoming research investigations in South West Africa could well be beneficial to both of their academic studies.

Christiane had to tell Charles that her father, Count Lüneberg, had always been rather suspicious about any person showing too much interest in her so, 'during our visit it is important for us not to show any of our affection for one another; we must even avoid holding hands in view of my parents.'

Charles had been rather overawed by the magnificence of Schloss Braunschweig, which had been the Lüneberg's family home since the mid-eighteenth century.

In August 2003, they were met by the Count's chauffeur at Hanover airport and driven to her home in an immaculately polished black Mercedes W201. After passing through the exquisite gateway and lodge, which was ringed by a colonnade, the half-mile tree-lined drive wound its way to the mansion itself. The building was symmetrical with corner turrets, mock battlements, bay windows and a turreted *porte cochière.*

The centrepiece of the large entrance hall was a magnificent imperial staircase framed by pairs of Corinthian columns, and the balustrades were highlighted by gilt and silver. The majority of the ornate high-ceilinged rooms on the ground floor were sumptuously furnished and oak-panelled. The library on the east wing of the mansion overlooked an immaculately tended formal garden, whereas the sitting room on the west wing focussed its view onto a green carpet of meadow sweeping down to an ornamental lake. Standing well back from the north of Schloss Braunschweig was a sizeable stable yard, with a clock tower, carriage houses, and adjacent to this was a small, domed, classical chapel which Christiane's parents and their household and estate workers attended each Sunday.

Charles was given a bedroom on the east wing of the building, which had rather sombre, dark-coloured walls and was furnished with a four-poster bed with curtains, a large wardrobe and a small writing desk and chair. All the family bedrooms were located far away in the west wing of the mansion. Although Charles and Christiane had slept together on a number of occasions, they had never consummated their relationship. For prior to sleeping together, Christiane had told Charles that although the Hanoverian region of her home in Germany was primarily of the Protestant faith, her family had always adhered to the teachings of the Roman Catholic Church, and that sex before marriage was very much *verboten*.

Therefore, as far as she was concerned, such carnal knowledge should only be given to the person that she would eventually choose to share the rest of her life as husband, and to have children with. So, even a romantic nocturnal get-together at Christiane's ancestral home had been certainly out of the question. Christiane had even been prevented from showing Charles the room where she had been born and raised, and her parents had ensured that he had to be kept well away from their family rooms in the western wing of the mansion.

After having spent almost a week at Schloss Braunschweig, and prior to their departure, Christiane told Charles that her parents would grant her permission to stay with him at his family home at Hartlington Hall in Yorkshire, and also, 'Although you do not have a Germanic background you acted as a gentleman throughout your time with them, and therefore no doubt you could be trusted to take good care of me, when we meet in Southern Africa. Thank goodness, they can see that actually it could be useful to both of us to share some of our research studies, so they are happy for us to meet in Africa.'

On hearing this, Charles was quick to take Christiane into his arms and to hug her, to kiss her on both cheeks and then warmly on her lips, before releasing her from his embrace.

Christiane's ten-day stay with Charles at Hartlington Hall could not have been more of a contrast to their time together at Schloss Braunschweig. For throughout her stay Christiane had found Charles's parents, Mathew and Jan Duncan, to be most welcoming, informal and for her to have always felt completely relaxed in their company. Almost as if they were already considering her to be another member of their close family.

Charles had decided to tell Christiane about the history of their family seat, and how its acquisition had been quite recent in comparison to her parents' inheritance. 'It was my great-grandfather, a successful mill owner in Bradford, who bought the 1,800-acre estate soon after he had bought a baronetcy, in 1914, at the start of the First World War. Sir Reginald Duncan's only son, my grandfather, Sir Colin Duncan, had two sons and a daughter. His eldest son, my Uncle Sebastian, is a colonel in the Life Guards of the Household Brigade and inherited the baronetcy after the death of my grandfather in 1982. My uncle is married but has no children.'

Charles explained to Christiane that his father, the younger brother, Mathew Duncan, was awarded a science PhD from Emory University in the US after having spent several years in Africa carrying out field studies with various different species of primates, including the eastern lowland gorilla in the Congo, and other primate species in Southern Rhodesia. He had met Charles's mother, Jan Labuschagne, in Rhodesia.

'My mother was born in South Africa to an old Afrikaner farming family in the Transvaal, then moved with her parents as a young girl to Southern Rhodesia in the late 1950s. She was first married to a senior officer in Rhodesia's Selous Scouts, who lost his life in the late 1970s during the Bush War. This was when they met and married in Rhodesia before she came to the UK – she'd never been here before. After my grandfather's death, my uncle wished to remain in the Household Cavalry so my father agreed to take over the running of the Hartlington Hall estate.'

Both Charles and Christiane had enjoyed horse riding from their formative years and they spent a great deal of their time during their stay galloping throughout the estate's Home Park, negotiating their way through the winding paths of the beech woods. On one occasion, Charles had taken Christiane for a picnic on a small island in the middle of the slow-flowing shallow waters of the River Wharfe, which had on its south side a backdrop of a thin line of trees which gave way to the heather-covered moors and hills of the Yorkshire Dales. To the north, on the crest of a hill, could be seen the splendour of the south façade of the eighteenth-century Queen Anne mansion of Hartlington Hall.

The Hall's resident cook, Mrs Francis Higgins, had prepared for them a game pie and a wedge of Wensleydale cheese. Charles toasted Christiane with a glass of Henkell Trocken and rather nervously said, 'Christiane, I am sure that you are now well aware how extremely fond I am of you, and I have been wondering whether once we have both finished our university degrees, do you think that you could ever marry me?'

Christiane had immediately blushed and, after having gently kissed him, said, 'Charles, let's just see what the next couple of years has in store for us, for I too am extremely fond of you but to be realistic I do not know enough about life at this stage to commit myself to anyone.'

They held each other tight and after a while Christiane broke free, and, with some moisture having gathered in her eyes, said, 'Let us just hope that our relationship will continue to blossom in the wonderful way that it has done, and that our future time together when we meet up in South West Africa will be as productive as ever.'

*

During Charles's last night in Gumare, he had managed to make contact with Christiane at Schloss Braunschweig. He could tell from her voice how excited she was to receive his call, and to hear the stories from his stay in Nxau Nxau. As they had previously made a pact to always tell each other almost everything about their respective lives, Charles had found it extremely difficult not to share with her the compromising circumstances that had given rise to the blackmail he was now having to deal with.

But he prevented himself from doing so for he could well imagine the reaction the Count and Countess of Lüneberg, if they ever had the slightest suspicion that there was a photograph circulating of the nude figure of their daughter's boyfriend, standing in front of a similarly naked young girl lying in bed with outstretched arms. For Charles well recognised that should such a rumour find its way to Schloss Braunschweig, this would put a total end to his ambition to one day ask the Count for his daughter's hand in marriage.

On his return to Nxau Nxau Charles was quick to make contact with Kisi again to see whether he had managed to receive any information about the identity of the person, or persons, who were blackmailing him, as well as to seek further guidance from him as to what to do next.

'Charles, although I have my suspicions, I have been unable to secure any real proof about the identity of the girl, or of the person or persons who are blackmailing you. However, my best advice to you is to inform Thopelo Riruako exactly what happened on the night in question, and to show him the note of blackmail along with its associated image of you and the girl. For as you already know, Thopelo is perhaps the most trusted tribal elder and friend of our chief.'

So, taking Kisi's advice, Charles had a meeting with Thopelo only three days prior to the deadline that he had been given to place the US $500 in the waste bin of his bathroom, and told him everything – that he had been awoken in the middle of the night and had experienced a young African girl climbing into his bed and attempting to embrace him, and how he had managed to immediately extricate himself from her grasp. Also, he described how he had jumped out of the bed, thrown a towel around himself and left the hut immediately to find Kisi. He showed Thopelo the image and the note of blackmail. 'I managed to find Kisi's *rondavel* and, prior to spending the rest of the night on the floor, I told him exactly what had occurred.'

Very much to Charles's surprise, Thopelo did not seem to be too concerned about what had taken place, presenting Charles in such a compromising way, and said, 'As you may know, Charles, as one of the chief's most senior elders, I am considered by some to represent the "eyes, ears and nose" of our village, and there is very little that escapes my attention. And, most regrettably, there are some bad elements in Nxau Nxau who resent your presence in their village, particularly you being so observant and asking so many questions about their lifestyles, as well as having been accepted by the majority of the chief's subjects. Therefore, with your permission, I would like to relate exactly what you have told me, and show both the blackmail note and the image of you and the girl to Chief Tjamuaha, for I feel confident that he will arrive at a satisfactory course of action.'

Charles mulled over this suggestion for a while before accepting it, as he had failed to arrive at any alternative option. He had considered that the worst scenario he could possibly be confronted with was for the chief to ask him to leave the village. And perhaps with the help of Tjipene, with his cousin Mothinsi in Maun, he could be found another location to continue his studies of the Herero dynasty.

The day after his meeting with Thopelo, Kisi had acted as a communication link between the tribal elders and Charles and had told him, 'It is considered best for you to be away from Nxau Nxau at the time of the deadline for you to respond to the blackmail request, so I have arranged for you to be taken by one of my younger brother's sons, Gabriel, on a field trip down to Lake Ngami for a few days. There, you will be able to meet other members of our Herero tribe tending their cattle in that particular area. However, prior to doing so, please leave this envelope in the waste bin in your bathroom, after which this blackmail matter will be attended to.'

Prior to leaving Charles had organised his camping equipment and supplies for the planned four to five days away from the village, as he had told Kisi that he would prefer to sleep in his tent instead of one of the village's *rondavels*. He made sure that before leaving he had with him all the notes that he had gleaned from Thopelo and others, for losing these should his hut be set on fire would mean his past month or so in Botswana had been a total waste of his time.

Lake Ngami was some 200 kilometres south of Gumare and the journey to Sehitwa, on the edge of the lake, took Gabriel about two and a half hours. Charles had previously read a good deal about the lake, which at the height of the rainy season covers an area of some seventy-two kilometres squared and the lake was only a few feet deep, rich in plankton, with a matted forest of oxygen-producing plants growing from its muddy bottom. Due to these water plants and the saltiness of the water from evaporation, the lake plays host to a high concentration and diversity of birdlife, which Charles was so looking forward to seeing. As well as being pleased to be well away from the village whilst the blackmail situation was being dealt with in some way or another.

One eloquent description of Lake Ngami he recalled reading was in Johnson, Bond and Bannister's book *Okavango: Sea of Land, Land of Water*:

> *From the lake shore it looks like a cloud of smoke, tossed by the wind, twisted into spirals in the sky. Then the smoke tumbles in a sunburst of wings, a spinning, flickering tornodo that marks the flight of the millions of birds dispersing from the water's edge. When the quelea [finches] are flying, it sounds as if rapids have appeared on the placid lake.*

Whereas Gabriel was accommodated by one of the villagers quite close to Sehitwa, Charles had decided to pitch his tent near to the lake, and he was provided with some charcoal to enable him to light a small fire to prepare his meals. During his time camped at the lakeside Charles was able to almost forget the compromising ramifications that had given rise to the cause of his blackmail, for his mind had been almost totally preoccupied by the profusion of the birdlife from greater and lesser flamingos, pink-backed pelicans, wood and sacred ibis, saddle-billed storks, spurwing geese, many different species of ducks and terns, blacksmith plovers to crested and wattled cranes. He was able to see how this was very much cattle country, as he passed four Africans wearing cowboy hats and riding agile-looking steeds, herding some 300 head of beef cattle away from the lake, where they had just refreshed themselves, to a nearby corral for the night.

In a letter to Christiane he wrote:

How very much I wish that you were with me here, for the birdlife could not be more spectacular, and the sunsets more breathtaking – the whole horizon becomes a vast red furnace into which the sun sinks like a fireball. Then in the evening a refreshing breeze wafts across the shallow waters of the lake, and the cloudless sky is alight with its galaxy of stars with the southern pole star being evident in proximity to the southern cross, and the birdlife becomes less noisy. Such a place, so entwined as it is with Mother Nature, could hardly be a more relaxing and enjoyable environment to experience. How very much I would love you to be sharing this with me now. I am already missing your company very much.

With my fondest love, Charles.

When Charles returned to the village, Kisi told him, 'Whilst you were enjoying the peaceful surroundings of Lake Ngami there has been quite a considerable disruption taking place around your base here. The police superintendent had arranged for a twenty-four-hour watch to take place by your house, and it has been subsequently reported that a teenage girl was captured by some unknown individuals, but not by the police, after having entered the rear of your dwelling in the early hours of Sunday morning. The police constable on duty at the time had told the superintendent that after he had heard a commotion he had gone to investigate, but had been just in time to see two men with a girl struggling between them, being dragged off into the darkness of the night.

'So, the police are anxious to know the identity of the two men, and the whereabouts of the girl that they had snatched from under the eyes of their constable. And the whole episode is presenting Kgosi with a mystery that he is becoming most concerned about, particularly that such an apparent kidnapping could possibly take place in his village. So, in order to prevent more rumours from circulating, he has decreed that anyone with knowledge of the blackmail that you have had to deal with must maintain such knowledge in the strictest of confidence, and therefore not to speak to others about it. For our chief does not wish it to be known that such kidnapping and blackmailing could possibly take place within this tribal territory.'

After having listened to all the information that Kisi had told him, Charles asked, 'Do you know what is likely to happen to the teenage girl? And do you consider that it is at all likely that the girl was the same person who had got into my bed?'

'I have no idea whether it is the same young lady or not, but please do take my advice that when you next have one of your meetings with Thopelo Riruako, do refrain from speaking about this matter with him,' Kisi replied. 'For I know how talking about such a subject would be of embarrassment to him.'

5

HORRORS OF WITCHCRAFT

Six weeks after Charles returned from Lake Ngami, the severed head of a teenage girl had been unearthed by a constable of the Botswana Police Service, from under the armchair of one of the chief's miner tribal elders, who lived in one of the smarter thatched dwelling in Nxau Nxau. For a couple of weeks before the find, a distraught lady from Nxau Nxau had travelled to Gumare to report to the police that her teenage niece had disappeared without any trace. And, as witchcraft is still practised in parts of Southern Africa, the police service in Botswana were anxious to do everything possible to bring those still resorting to the occult power of the supernatural to justice which, after a tip-off, had resulted in a constant police presence in the village, leading to the ultimate finding of the buried head.

Charles would have liked nothing more than to discuss this matter further with Kisi, but he fully recognised that either to broach the subject, or to speak about the girl's disappearance with him, could get them both into trouble. The chief's proclamation to restrict the spreading of rumours about kidnapping and the previous attempt to blackmail him was considered by those in the know to be totally binding. The next time Charles visited Gumare, he took his laptop with him, where he was able to do an internet search to satisfy his curiosity and find out for himself about the various ramifications of witchcraft, and the likelihood that the head found in his village could have been the consequence of occult practices.

Charles found that the government of Botswana had updated the country's original 1928 Witchcraft Act, legislating for the provision of punishment of any persons practising witchcraft, only as recently as 1998. Thereby, a person found guilty of an alleged crime that caused injury, disease, damage to property, torture, mutilation, death or to put any person in fear by supernatural means to produce any natural phenomena, including charms from body parts, and associated medicines commonly used, would be prosecuted.

The Act outlawed sorcery, enchantment, bewitching, the use of instruments of witchcraft, the purported exercise of any occult power, and the possession and passing on of any occult knowledge. Concluding that any person who employs or solicits any other person to resort to the use of witchcraft, or possesses any instrument of witchcraft for any purpose, would be committing a crime.

In the past witchcraft had caused tribal uprisings, even wars, and had given rise to murders caused by mutilation, which involved taking the soft parts of the body like heart, liver, kidneys, and having them all crushed up and spread over land prior to planting mealies (maize) in September and October, in order to enrich crops. In one of the recorded cases, when a local witchdoctor had made too many bad prophecies, he had been beaten up, set on fire and burnt to death. In more recent times when HIV had become a particularly serious problem in the villages, infidelity was becoming increasingly frowned upon. Witchdoctors had been known to place a death curse on those ladies who were purported to have in the first case transmitted the disease, despite the fact that so much of the HIV infection was being spread by men, who were never cursed in such a way.

There had been one particular case recorded that highlighted this practice. A young woman who was accused by a witchdoctor of having usurped some of his supernatural powers by luring menfolk to her bed had been murdered; her body parts were strewn around a nearby plot of mealies. Despite lengthy police service investigation, after the villagers had adopted a 'Cloak of Uncooperative Silence' the culprit, or culprits, were never found or prosecuted for such a gruesome murder. After reading this account, Charles just wondered whether those responsible for the disappearance of the teenage girl in Nxau Nxau would ever be found.

During this stay in Gumare, Charles had met up again with Zhang Jinchu at the Makgovango Luxury Inn and had been keen to tell him all about the wonderful few days that he had recently spent camped on the shores of Lake Ngami.

Zhang's response to this was, 'I have heard reports that a head of a young woman has been found at the village where you are based, and that the police are very anxious to find out the identity of the youth concerned. Also, I have been told that a lady from your village had recently been in contact with the police in Gumare about the unexplained disappearance of one of her nieces. All of these events sound most intriguing to me, for according to some of the rumours I've heard the severed head was the consequence of a mutilation decreed by a witchdoctor, who lives in a village to the west of Nxau Nxau. Also, Charles, are you able to tell me anything else about it that you might have heard in the village? For it all sounds such a tragic and horrible end to a young person's life. And it would be interesting to know what star the victim came under.'

Charles would have loved to tell Zhang all about the blackmail, the subsequent kidnap of an unidentified girl who had entered his dwelling in the early hours of the morning and had since disappeared without a trace. But he knew only too well of the consequences if he told Zhang anything which leaked back to Kgosi.

He therefore responded, 'Zhang, there is currently quite an intense police service investigation being carried out in the village, and in order to avoid more sensational rumours from circulating as to what may or may not be connected with the decapitated head, it has been decreed that all talk on this subject is banned for the time being. I was away at Lake Ngami at the time of the head's discovery, so I have nothing to add other than to say that the police are doing as much as possible to resolve this matter at the earliest opportunity.'

The rest of their evening's conversation was very much about what progress Zhang was making with regards to his meetings with local tribesmen in his quest to secure permission to search for minerals on their respective tribal lands. He mentioned to Charles, 'Quite recently I managed to overhear two elderly Africans, whom I have seen here in the bar on a number of occasions before, talking about how they had just been in conversation with a Japanese national who had been making enquiries about mineral deposits in the area. As soon as I heard Nxau Nxau mentioned, I managed to move slightly closer to their table in order to hear more clearly what they were talking about. I heard them say that they had showed the Japanese man a mineral deposit that they had dug out from land quite close to your village, and how the Japanese man had remained talking to them for the remainder of the evening.'

Zhang had been particularly anxious to know the identity of the two Africans with the mineral samples. He told Charles, 'As I knew that they were regular visitors to the bar, I described them both to the barman, and after having given him a US $50 note I asked him to find out their names and as much about them as possible. I told him that if he were successful in doing this, he would be given a further dollar note for his services.

'A couple of days later I returned to the bar and, after having handed the barman a second US $50 note, he told me that the two Africans which I had asked him about come into the bar each weekend and are elders of the village of Nxau Nxau, which is about two hours' drive to the west of us here, and their names are Jefta Kandorozu and Megano Angelo. And after a further query, the barman added that the Japanese man is called Katsuro Khama and his business card records that he is from the Japan Oil, Gas, Metal and Diamond Corporation. When he comes to the Inn he often buys drinks for people that he has not met before, then seems to engage himself in quite lengthy conversations with them. I have recently been told by one of the people he has spoken to that he is particularly interested in hearing about any rumours with regards to mineral deposits in the region, and will reward handsomely any person who could lead him to the locality of such.'

After Zhang had described the two Africans to Charles, he could not help reflecting how their descriptions reminded him of the two sullen-looking tribal elders from Nxau Nxau, who had refused to shake hands with him. However, after they finished their evening by having a meal together at the Makgovango Inn, Charles promised that on his return to his village he would try to find out as much as possible about Jefta Kandorozu and Megano Angelo.

'Zhang, I think that in future it is important for us to share as much information as possible about what could be underhand clandestine dealings between the two elders and Katsuro Khama,' Charles ventured. 'So, let us arrange to meet in a fortnight's time during my next visit, and we can discuss any further information that we may have managed to collect on the three people concerned.'

Although Zhang had been happy to agree to this suggestion, he did not wish to divulge to his new friend that he too would be very interested to negotiate with the two African elders about acquiring rights to explore for minerals. Even if this were to mean having to outbid and double-cross the Japanese operator in acquiring such mineral rights, as well as the possibility of acquiring from them any mineral samples that they may have in their personal possession, which they would be willing to offer him on a mutually beneficial basis.

On Charles's return to Nxau Nxau he continued to have his regular meetings with Thopelo Riruako, to learn as much as possible about the traditions of his tribe. He would compare these traditions with those of their ancestors in Namibia, when he had discussions with the Herero tribesmen there in a few months' time. With his new interest in African witchcraft, he had been particularly interested to hear about the many medicinal resources that the Hereros manage to collect from the surrounding vegetation to act as remedies for respiratory disorders, constipation, diarrhoea and many other ailments.

Thopelo had told him, 'Sometimes teenage girls will present a gift to a family who claim to have supernatural powers, so that they choose the right husband for her and guarantee many healthy children with him. Also, some people give gifts in order to guide the weather, and even to bring on the rains and improve the state of the harvest.' When Charles had asked Thopelo whether there were any witchdoctors practising such a cult in this region of Botswana, he had been quick to respond that witchcraft had been outlawed in Botswana for many decades.

At the time of Chief Tjamuaha's next monthly Saturday morning meeting under the shade of the vast baobab tree, he had observed the two elders, Jefta and Megano, in deep conversation with one another, standing behind Kgosi. Although there had been many lengthy questions put forward to the chief, and equally long responses from him, none of these came from the two elders that Charles was most interested in.

As Kisi was the person in the village that Charles felt most at ease to talk to, at their next meeting he said, 'Kisi, I think that

I have previously mentioned to you that soon after my arrival here, when Kgosi introduced me to your tribal elders, how two of those gathered had refused to shake my hand and had avoided any eye contact with me. I can now identify them as Jefta Kandorozu and Megano Angelo. Could you tell me something about their background, and their relationship with the chief?'

'Charles, as we have become good friends during your time in my village, and we've shared quite a number of confidentialities, I trust that what I now tell you, you will keep to yourself, and certainly not relate to any other member of my tribe,' Kisi replied. As Charles was only too happy to agree with this request, he continued, 'Both Jefta and Megano are second cousins to Kgosi, but have never got on well with him, and in the past there has been a number of rumours about how they had been plotting to undermine the chief's powers. These had been thwarted due to the general popularity of Kgosi.'

On hearing about this gulf between the two elders and their chief, Charles decided to let Kisi know something about his meeting with Zhang in Gumare, and how Zhang had told him about the meetings of Jefta and Megano at the Makgovango Luxury Inn with a Japanese dealer in valuable gemstones. Although Charles decided not to tell Kisi about them having found some mineral deposits near Nxau Nxau, he asked, 'Are you aware of any evidence or rumours of minerals having been found recently near to your village and, if so, would Jefta and Megano be the elders responsible, on behalf of your tribe, for dealing with such matters?'

Kisi's response to Charles's question was, 'Certainly not.'

Remembering well his discussions with Colin Patterson in Gaberone and with Mothinsi in Maun, and how he had promised to pass on any information about Chinese or Japanese nationals scanning the country for mineral exploration, he decided to provide Mothinsi's cousin Tjipene with all the information that he had acquired to date.

This information was delivered to Tjipene, as had been previously arranged, via a packet of cigarettes with Charles having written a short summary of the situation providing the names of the two Herero elders, as well as the name of the Japanese gemstone negotiator, although he had been unable to find out the name, or the names, of the Japanese mineral corporation(s) that he was selling the valuable gems to. Although at this stage of giving the information, Charles had decided not to mention Zhang's particular background. The note was given to Tjipene after he was leaving the monthly morning meeting of elders, when Charles offered him a cigarette and invited him to keep the rest of the packet.

The police service presence in Nxau Nxau had become more intense, and Charles could sense how the inspector was becoming greatly frustrated by the 'cloak of silence' that he had found throughout the village, after they had received the tip-off about the young girl's severed head. Charles had overheard a conversation confirming the rumour that the head had been found under the chair of one of the villagers, who was visiting relatives some distance away at the time of its discovery.

Unknown to Charles, prior to his next visit to Gumare, Zhang had contacted his father, Li Yang, at his base in Kitwe in the Zambian Copperbelt. He had given him all the information that he had managed to collect about the Japanese precious gemstone negotiator, and how the man had appeared to also be negotiating mineral exploration rights in a clandestine fashion with two tribal elders from a nearby village of the Herero tribe. Zhang's father had immediately responded by instructing his son to continue to find out as much as possible about such negotiations and, ideally, to attempt to identify the mineral sample that had been offered. He had told Zhang to determine as precisely as possible the geographical location of where the mineral deposit had been found, and in the meantime he would investigate through his network of agents the background and general effectiveness of Katsuro Khama as an operator.

Five days after Charles had provided Tjipene with the information that he had gathered, he found a cigarette packet under his pillow with a response from Mothinsi in Maun. The message read:

> *I received your message safely. It has recently been reported that some foreign corporations have started to use satellite survey technology without having obtained the government's formal permission in order to gain an advance on other mineral corporations operating in Botswana. And as you are already aware, Botswana has many mineral resources, such as diamonds, silver, copper, iron, nickel and soda ash. However, there are still many unexplored other mineral resources that are to be found in remote areas below the sands of the Kalahari, such as gypsum, asbestos, chromium, graphite and manganese, and even sometimes diamonds and deposits of iron ore can be discovered in these areas. However, between seventy to eighty per cent of the country's earnings are attributed to diamond mining, which play a dominant role in Botswana's economy. Therefore, please do everything possible to find out the identity of the mineral deposits that are being offered by the two Herero tribal elders, for such information would be invaluable for us to investigate further.*

When the time came for Charles's next fortnightly visit to Gumare, he was feeling in two minds as to how much he should divulge to Zhang about his real motivation for learning as much as possible about the Japanese operator, and his meetings with the two tribal elders. For he could not help feeling that Zhang too had an alternative motive in gaining as much information as possible about their interactions. So, he decided to remain silent as to how he had conveyed all the information about the meeting of Katsuro Khama with the two Herero elders, and how he was acting as a conduit of such data via Tjipene and Mothinsi, to a member of the UK secret service in Gaberone.

At their usual meeting place in the bar of the Makgovango Inn, Zhang said, 'The barman has provided me with some further information about Katsuro Khama, in that he has not been into the bar or seen around Gumare for some time. Also, that the two elders from Nxau Nxau have been making enquiries into his whereabouts, for they are anxious to make contact with him again. The most recent information he has managed to collect is that Katsuro booked out of the hostel where he had been staying and had not left any evidence as to where he had gone. Evidently, the reason for the tribal elders' anxiety was that Katsuro had departed with the mineral sample that they had left with him to identify and value, which they had considered to be a very high-quality gemstone.'

'I have made enquiries in the village about Jefta and Megano, and they certainly are not undertaking anything official on behalf of the village's tribal chief, Moagi Tjamuaha,' Charles responded. 'It's evident that they are acting in a clandestine manner in their attempt to personally benefit from providing foreigners with mineral exploration rights in Nxau Nxau. Despite both Jefta and Megano being second cousins to Kgosi, they have been trying to undermine his authority for several years and are therefore considered by most to be undesirable people to become involved with. No doubt, due to their underhand dealings with a foreigner, they have not made any contact with the police service in Gumare either about Katsuro's disappearance or the theft of their mineral sample.'

'I very much doubt it,' Zhang replied.

During dinner, Zhang asked Charles again about the many rumours that were in circulation regarding the severed head of the girl being found, but as the last thing Charles wanted to get back to the village was that he was the source of rumours connected with the girl's disappearance, all he said was, 'The police are currently constantly present in Nxau Nxau in their attempt to locate the rest of the girl's body, and to possibly find the identity of the culprit, or culprits, of such a gruesome murder, and that is all I am able to tell you.'

As Zhang had the feeling that Charles was hiding some information from him about this matter, he asked whether he had any idea who in the village would have been responsible for the crime or why. 'Is there any evidence that the murder and decapitation was the result of a witchdoctor's spell?'

'I doubt it, for witchcraft has been banned in Botswana for many years,' Charles tactfully replied. 'Although there has been some recent evidence that it is still being practised in some of the more outlying areas. But during my many conversations with the people in the village about their tribal traditions, there has never been any mention that witchcraft is still being practised.'

They had ended their evening together agreeing to keep in touch and to share any further information on the whereabouts of Katsuro Khama. Charles had considered it worthwhile to tell Zhang that the two elders from Nxau Nxau were the same two who had refused to shake hands at their initial meeting.

Some ten days after Charles's return to the village, the dismembered body of a girl had been dug up from the midst of a large stand of elephant grass behind the small thatched classroom. The site had been found by some children who had been playing hide and seek within the maze of tall elephant grass, and had wondered why quite a large patch of the grass had been so trampled upon, and why some of the earth beneath its roots had looked so disturbed. So, as a consequence, two of the boys had told one of their teachers who, in turn, had reported it to a visiting policeman.

When Kisi's nephew, Gabriel, drove Charles to a small settlement of his tribe to the south-east of Nxau Nxau, he had some news.

'Please do not mention to anybody back in the village what I am about to tell you, not even to my uncle who I know you see a great deal of, but the dismembered body has been identified as the seventeen-year-old Esther Ochuros, the girl who had been reported to the police to have disappeared by her aunt, just over a month ago.'

Charles was overwhelmed with anger against whoever had committed this brutality. 'Who on earth can be responsible for this? I assure you this will remain strictly between ourselves. It's appalling to think someone from the village could be responsible.'

'The girl had been one of the young ladies who had been hiring out their bodies for recreational sex, in the house that you are now living in, which was shut down just prior to your arrival due to infections that some of them were transmitting to their clients. However, according to the police inspector, Esther's dismembered body represented a typical occult murder by, or on the instruction of, a witchdoctor. For her decapitated corpse was found to have a bicycle spoke driven into her heart, and some of her internal organs had been removed. Also, as I believe you already know, her head was found buried under the seat of a respected member of our tribe.'

Charles was unsettled by the thought it had been his hut that the girl had been taken from.

'The man in question has never claimed to possess any supernatural powers,' Gabriel continued, 'and is certainly not a witchdoctor, so we consider that the girl's head had been placed under his chair in order for him to be implicated in her murder, and thereby for him to be subsequently accused and convicted. The police were anonymously informed about the head's location and have been unable to find any trace of who told them.'

After Charles had returned to Nxau Nxau and had written notes on the discussions he had had with some of the villagers at the nearby settlement, with Gabriel having acted as his translator, he had been dropped off at Thopelo Riruako's house. He had particularly wanted to check with Thopelo a number of his more recent recordings about the traditions of his Herero tribal dynasty. Also to show him a summary of some of his findings which he had just completed, prior to submitting a paper about these, for possible publication in the respected *International Journal of Anthropology and Ethnology*. It had not been to his surprise that Thopelo had made no mention of the corpse of the missing girl, or that her head had been recently located.

A couple of days later, after entering his dwelling, Charles was surprised to find a police inspector with one of his officers examining his clothing and other possessions. The police inspector apologised for the intrusion but told him that Chief Tjamuaha had given him, and his team, full permission to enter any of the houses/*rondavels* in Nxau Nxau without the necessity of a warrant or having first informed the occupant about their intended presence.

Charles's papers were scattered around the room and his belongings strewn across the floor; he was furious to find this level of disruption without having even been asked permission to enter. 'Whatever is the reason for you examining my possessions in the way that you are doing and causing such an upheaval in my room here? Also, why have you been examining my personal and most valuable academic files? For as the chief welcomed me to his village as "an honoured guest" I find it quite deplorable that you have entered my dwelling without first informing me of your intention.'

'You won't be aware of this but the body of the missing girl has been found and identified, and prior to your arrival at Nxau Nxau the same person spent a number of weeks with other young ladies, using the dwelling where you are now accommodated as what could be termed correctly as a brothel. We have also been told, which could of course be a rumour, that soon after your arrival in the village the same girl was observed entering this room in the early hours of the morning when you were in residence. Is this correct?'

Charles thought for a while before responding and having come to the conclusion that as the inspector had already gleaned so much information about the girl, it would be better to tell him about the entire blackmail scenario, for no doubt the chief had already told him about what his close confidant, Thopelo Riruako, had shown him concerning his involvement with the girl on the night in question. So, Charles sat down on the only chair in the room and related to the inspector exactly what had occurred on the night, and described the faded image of them both, and the subsequent note of blackmail.

'After these unfortunate events and the blackmail demand for US $500 had taken place, I was advised by an influential member of the tribe not to comply with the blackmail demand to pay any money to them. Therefore, not to leave an envelope enclosing the dollars in a waste bin in the bathroom here, which I had been requested to do. But instead, I was asked to leave an empty envelope in the waste bin. And as soon as I had complied with this suggestion, a five-day trip had been arranged for me to visit the wonders of Lake Ngami. Therefore, it was only on my return from the lake that I was informed that an unidentified girl had been caught leaving my bathroom in the early hours of the morning, with the envelope in her hand, and having been taken away by two unidentified men, has not been seen since.'

Charles rose from his chair and looked the inspector in the eye. 'That, Inspector, is all that I am able to tell you about this tragic situation, although I am obviously anxious to know whether Esther Ochuros was the same person who had, uninvited, entered my bed on the night in question? I gave the chief a copy of the blackmail letter, and the faded image of me standing by the bed, but I am not aware of what further information the chief may have about the subsequent disappearance of the girl in question. It may well be that those concerned were involved with the kidnapping of the girl, and possibly her gruesome murder. They may well be the same people who attempted to blackmail me for a sizeable sum of money, and, should I have failed to comply with their demand, to have humiliated me by circulating the image of my naked body standing by a bed, towering over a young lady who had her arms outstretched, to welcome me into her embrace. This would have resulted in me having to leave Nxau Nxau in disgrace.'

'I am sorry, Mr Charles, but I was provided with this information by promising total confidentiality,' the inspector responded. 'I shall certainly bear in mind the suspicions that you have just presented. However, I hope you will not mind, but in compliance with normal police procedure when carrying out such murder investigations, I should like the constable here to take a set of your fingerprints?' Charles was surprised at this request but felt that he had no alternative but to comply.

6

RUFFIANS AND ROUGH DIAMONDS

After the disappearance of Katsuro Khama from Gumare, seemingly along with the valuable mineral sample that Jefta Kandorozu and Megano Angelo had given to him to identify, Charles decided to further investigate the possibility of there being some valuable mineral deposits in Nxau Nxau, and whether there was any information that diamonds had previously been found in this region of Botswana. He planned to keep as close an eye as possible on the movements of both Jefta and Megano, and to find out more about them.

Charles had been told that there were many mineral stones that look like diamonds, having many similar physical characteristics so the finder can never be sure whether their transparent stone is the real thing. To correctly identify the mineral sample concerned, the person would have to have access to a sophisticated diamond-testing device, which works by passing electricity or heat through the stone in order to detect its conductivity. And he was told that diamonds in their rough or raw state, uncut and unpolished, look like transparent stones which are either colourless, tinted yellow or have a brownish colour. That is why the few colourless ones to be found are the most valuable and in the highest demand. They undergo the polishing and cutting process that produces their magnificent glitter.

Unknown to Charles, back in Gumare, Zhang had been active in following his father's request to do as much as possible to find out the whereabouts of Katsuro Khama, and whether he still had the mineral sample from Nxau Nxau. Also, Zhang's father had notified one of his subversive mining associates working for the Sanchuan Huanton Corporation International in Botswana to locate Katsuro, and if he still had the mineral sample, which from all reports was of high value, to steal it from him by any means. For Li Yang had no intention of a possible high-value mineral find in Botswana slipping out of the possible control and participation of the Jinchu family, without either of their respective Chinese mineral corporations having been involved.

Li Yang's associate, Huang, had first reported back to him in Kitwe that Katsuro was on his way to De Beer's in order to have the sample comprehensively evaluated. He had been informed by a prospector, who had already examined the stone on his portable diamond tester, that the sample was not a laboratory-grown synthetic one, was of a considerable size, had no hints of either yellow or brown and therefore could be of significant value. Li Yang decided not to inform his son about this information, but rather sent Huang an urgent message to take possession of the sample at the earliest opportunity, particularly prior to it being seen by diamond geologists at Debswana, the De Beers Botswana mining corporation headquarters in Gaberone. And Li Yang had added as an incentive that should Huang be successful with the stone's acquisition, he would be rewarded handsomely for his services, even being offered a percentage of the gemstone's ultimate value.

Huang had finally tracked down Katsuro at the Cresta Riley's Hotel in Maun, the day prior to him having booked to fly down to Gaberone to visit the offices of Debswana. Whilst enjoying an evening drink on the hotel's veranda, and the refreshing breeze coming up from the Thamalakane River below, Huang could see Katsuro sitting at a table in deep conversation with an attractive young African lady. He could see that it was the same girl who had earlier on in the afternoon approached him to enquire whether he would like to have a personal massage from her. As he had declined such an intimate offer, the girl had obviously moved on to solicit other more agreeable hotel guests. So, over Huang's second Castle lager he hatched a plan that he was later to put into effect.

Huang had found out the girl's name, Tonata, and her contact number from the hotel's receptionist. So, just before dinner Huang gave her a call and told her that whatever her fee was for the night, he would be willing to pay her double if she carried out a favour for him. This, he made it clear to her, was not to have her spend the night with him, but rather to do something special for him.

He arranged to meet her in his room, where he explained, 'I have seen that you have been spending quite some time with the Japanese gentleman staying here, and the way that you both said goodbye to one another before he went into dinner, I am of the opinion that you will be joining him in his bedroom later on in the evening.'

The young lady just nodded, and Huang continued, 'What I would like you to do, for the money that I shall be giving you, is that after he has enjoyed your attentions, you slip this strong sedative into the glass of whisky that you are to take with you. And for you to let me know as soon as you have left his room. The sedative is totally safe for you to administer, for it will merely put the gentleman into a deep slumber for a couple of hours or more.'

Just after midnight, Tonata had come to Huang's room to tell him that the gentleman had drained the doctored glass of whisky with the dissolved capsule, and he was now snoring his head off in bed. Huang handed the young lady a wad of mixed banknotes as had been requested, Botswana pulas and American dollars, and after she had carefully checked the amount that had been promised, she hurried from his bedroom. After which Huang took every care not to be seen by any other of the hotel guests or staff members as he walked as quietly as possible along the dimly lit corridor to Katsuro's room to search for the gemstone. And, as the 'lady of the night' had told him, he found the Japanese man snoring and in evident deep sleep.

As Huang was well aware that the hotel did not provide security safes in the hotel bedrooms, he knew that the gem must be hidden in some part of Katsuro's room. So, he first made a search of the contents of his jacket and trousers, which included his wallet and various other items found in the pockets. Unable to find any evidence of the gemstone having been stitched into either Katsuro's jacket or trousers, or into the clothes hanging up in the wardrobe, he followed the same procedure in carefully examining the contents of his suitcase, feeling for any unexpected lumps, searching for any secret pockets in the case, but to no avail.

When Huang carefully examined the dark grey panama, which had been hanging on a hook on the back of the door, he felt something quite hard under the bow of the hatband, and it was then that he had found what he had been seeking. However, prior to leaving the bedroom, with Katsuro still snoring seemingly as happily as ever, he left a preconceived typed note wrapped around a small stone in a cellophane capsule, which he placed in the panama's hatband. The note simply read: *'When you read this, the gemstone which you stole from the Herero tribe has now been taken out of Botswana, and this warns you to never attempt to locate its whereabouts.'*

The following morning Huang was pleased to see Katsuro enjoying his breakfast and soon afterwards, as if he hadn't a care in the world, depart with his suitcase and panama to Maun's airport. Hopefully, Katsuro would not discover that his precious gemstone had been exchanged for a valueless stone and the attached message before he extracted them from the hatband, just prior to his appointment at the Debswana headquarters.

It took just over a week for Zhang's father to send him a coded message to inform him that the Nxau Nxau gemstone was now safely in his possession. And that as Zhang had told him about Katsuro Khama having absconded with the gem that Jefta Kandorozu and Angelo Megano had lent him to assess, once he had had it fully valued a generous percentage of the sale price would be placed into his CITIC Ka Wah Bank account in Hong Kong.

Li Yang had added in his coded message:

Please, as discreetly as possible, make contact with the two tribal elders when they next visit Gumare. For once they are aware that you are a representative of a major Chinese mineral corporation dealing in gemstones, they may well take you into their confidence about their initial find, and possibly engage into conversation with you with regards to potentially offering you similar rough diamonds to that of our prize.

*

During the next conversation that Charles had with Thopelo Riruako he was surprised to learn that the police service had placed Jefta Kandorozu under house arrest, that he had a police constable stationed outside his dwelling and was forbidden to receive any visitors after dark.

Thopelo had said, 'The reason for Jefta's arrest was that Kgosi had received a message, via Gumare, from the Embassy of Japan in Gaberone. It had been reported to them by one of their Japanese compatriots that there could be a valuable mineral deposit to be found in Nxau Nxau. And that Jefta Kandorozu had been named by an informer as being directly involved in an attempted clandestine sale of what was considered a valuable rough gemstone. The Japanese ambassador considered it was important for our chief to be informed there could be a valuable mineral deposit around Nxau Nxau, and that a senior elder was attempting to steal from his fellow Hereros what should rightfully be for all of the community to benefit from.'

'Does Jefta admit his involvement?'

'He has fiercely denied having any knowledge of mineral deposits being found or having any involvements in attempting to sell a valuable gemstone. As the chief had received this information from an influential foreign embassy in Gaberone, he concluded that the report must have been based on the truth. So, Kgosi decided to take immediate action and showed the Japanese ambassador's letter to the police superintendent in charge of investigating Esther Ochuros's murder, which resulted in Jefta's immediate house arrest.'

Later in the same week, while Gabriel was driving Charles to another small settlement for him to talk to people about their inherited traditions and current lifestyles, he passed on some further confidential information.

'It has now been determined that the murdered girl, Esther Ochuros, is a niece of Jefta Kandorozu, that it is well known that Esther had never liked her uncle, for it had been rumoured that as a child, she had been molested by him and, as a consequence, had always been scared of him and appeared to be under his control. However, the rumours that are now gathering force suggest that Esther could have known the whereabouts of the purported mineral deposits, and that she may have been about to inform our chief, or one of his senior elders, about the location and perhaps even something about her uncle's clandestine dealings with a Japanese foreigner in Gaberone.'

After being told this, Charles wondered whether – if it had been Esther Ochuros who had climbed into his bed – she had been forced to do so by Jefta in order for the blackmail to take place. Charles considered that after the blackmail had failed and with Jefta's aim thwarted, if Esther had informed on Jefta his reputation would have been so compromised it could have resulted in him being requested to leave Nxau Nxau for good. With Esther's possible coerced involvement, had her knowledge of the incidents leading up to the blackmail also represented a danger for her?

Charles had already come to the conclusion that from his first meetings with both Jefta and Megano, they had resented his presence in their village. This could well have been due to Kgosi having made it known that Charles wanted to speak to as many villagers as possible during his time with them all. So, Jefta and Megano could well have jumped to the conclusion that during his meetings with the villagers, he could possibly hear something about their clandestine dealings with foreigners from outside their village, which would have been the very last thing that they wanted. Also, they both may have considered that his real presence in their village was possibly as a police informer, and the case that he was an anthropologist studying the traditions of their Herero heritage was a mere 'front'.

For Charles, everything now seemed to be making some sense. He had once again found a cigarette packet under his pillow, obviously placed there by Tjipene, which had contained a short message from Mothinsi. The message read:

It has come to the notice of Pat… in Gab… that a Japanese mineralogist, who had previously resided in Gumare, has recently had a valuable rough diamond stolen from him

> *on his way to have it correctly assessed and valued at the headquarters of Debswana in Gab... Could the Japanese gentleman be Katsuro Khama, who you referred to in your previous communication, or is Khama still residing in Gumare?*

Charles had also heard fresh rumours in the village that the police were now working on the supposition that Jefta Kandorozu had possibly arranged for a witchdoctor from a nearby village to cast a death spell on his niece, which had resulted in her gruesome murder, her subsequent decapitation and the removal of her body parts. And that her head had been placed under the chair of a known arch enemy of Jefta Kandorozu's in order to implicate him with her murder. Although what Jefta had evidently not known at the time of the murder was that his enemy had been away from the village, visiting relatives, for quite some time.

However, Charles was pleased to have confirmed by the police superintendent that it was indeed Kandorozu's niece, Esther Ochuros, who had got into his bed on the night in question. Charles could now clearly see the pieces of the jigsaw coming together. Although the very thought of the way that Esther had been murdered and her body had been disposed of had started to give him nightmares.

During Charles's next visit to Gumare he had a further meeting with Zhang. The news about Jefta had clearly spread.

'Charles, there is much talk in Gumare about Jefta Kandorozu having been placed under house arrest with a constant police guard on his dwelling. It has been suggested that Kandorozu was connected to a witchdoctor from a nearby village who invoked a death curse on the unfortunate girl. Also, it has been established that the murdered girl was Jefta's niece and that, it is rumoured, he had almost supernatural powers over her. Are these all true?'

'I'm in no position to confirm whether they are true but there is talk of little else in the village,' Charles replied. 'It seems scarcely credible that one of the trusted elders has been charged with such an atrocious crime.'

'Also, there are more rumours circulating about there being some valuable mineral deposits having been found in the vicinity of Nxau Nxau; have you been able to find out anything more about this? For, if not, I would very much like the opportunity for you to introduce me to Chief Tjamuaha and through negotiation with him, on behalf of the Bazhong Hangheng Plc that I represent, to obtain the sole mineral exploration rights for the lands that come under the chief's jurisdiction.'

Charles had hesitated for a while, during which time Zhang had gone to the bar to buy a second round of Castle lagers. After Zhang had placed the two pint glasses on the corner table, which was well out of earshot of nearby customers, Charles responded to Zhang's suggestion.

'As I feel sure you are already aware, I hold the chief in great respect, and I would never act in any way to deceive him or do anything that would be to the detriment of his Herero people. However, providing it would be your corporation's intentions, during any possible future negotiations that you may have with Chief Tjamuaha, that you will deal with him totally fairly, and that providing the results of any agreement that may be arrived at between you and Kgosi will be to the ultimate benefit of his tribe, I can see no reason why I should not agree to your request to introduce you to the chief.'

Prior to the two of them parting, Charles said, 'Zhang, over the past few months we have had many conversations on a great number of topics. However, although we have become good friends during our meetings here in Gumare, I hope that you will forgive me for asking you to give me your solemn word that in any future dealings that you may have with the chief, your agreements will always be to the maximum benefit for the future welfare of his Herero tribe?' Zhang had hesitated slightly prior to shaking hands with Charles and providing him with the assurance that he had requested.

*

Back in Nxau Nxau, Charles had noticed that since the house arrest of Jefta, his close friend Megano Angelo had been nowhere to be seen in the village, and that his small dwelling appeared to be deserted. However, unknown to Charles, Zhang had spotted Megano in Gumare's market purchasing some fish and had managed to engage in conversation with him after buying him a drink at a small stall nearby. And during his talk with Megano he told him that he represented a large Chinese mineral corporation which were seeking to purchase minerals in the area, no matter what quality or quantity they may represent. And Megano had been quick to respond to Zhang's enquiry by telling him that he was in possession of three rough diamonds and, as he was about to travel to Namibia to visit some of his ancestors, was seeking to make a quick sale.

Subsequent to their discussions they had arranged to meet again that evening, and at the meeting, although Megano did not allow the samples to be taken out of his sight, Zhang had managed to improvise a diamond-testing device with which he examined the stones. And after leaving the room to make a coded phone call to his father in Kitwe, he was able to return to make Megano a reasonable cash offer for the three samples of rough diamonds, which he had been quick to accept. At twelve noon the following day, the cash in both US dollars and in Botswana pulas was handed over to Megano. Before he left for the airport, Zhang had given Megano his contact numbers and address and told him that should he become involved in any future undercover sale of gemstones, or mineral rights, to please make contact with him. For he was sure that they would be able to negotiate a worthwhile financial deal to their mutual benefit.

Zhang had been happy to have been relieved of the sizeable amount of banknotes, and to have returned to his room and let his father know that the rough diamonds were now safely in his possession. And during his conversation, he had asked his father to provide him with a full description of the person that he was to hand over the minerals to. He had suggested to his father that the recipient would have to give him a pre-arranged password, so that no mistakes could possibly be made.

*

Two weeks after Megano Angelo's departure for Namibia, Charles had arranged the meeting between Zhang and Chief Moagi Tjamuaha. Prior to the meeting, Charles had given Kgosi Zhang's professional background, had vouched for his integrity and had explained his wish to investigate the rumour that some valuable mineral deposits were to be found within his tribal lands. He had explained that if Zhang was to establish any positive evidence of there being some worthwhile mineral deposits, he would wish to negotiate a formal contract between Bazhong Hangheng Plc and the chief, in order for his company to have the sole investigatory mineral mining rights.

At the meeting, at which some of Kgosi's most trusted elders were also present, he said, 'Should this company manage to locate a viable quantity of mineral deposits, probably by using some of the most up-to-date satellite survey technology, after the initial cost of locating the deposits has been recovered the contract between the chief and his company would guarantee that further profits would be shared on a highly advantageous basis for the Herero tribal people.'

After having put forward this proposition to Chief Tjamuaha and his closest tribal elders, it had been received with a considerable degree of enthusiasm by them all. So, on Zhang's drive back to Gumare, his mind was very much preoccupied by his consideration that, on the one hand, he had no intention of going back on his pledge to Charles to not do anything to deceive the chief in any way, but at the same time he needed to work out the best way to cream off some of the revenue derived from the contract, without the knowledge of his employees at their headquarters in Namibia.

It was during this time that Charles had one of his last meetings with Thopelo Riruako, who had provided him with so much invaluable information about the background and customs of his Herero tribe. And as Charles had not previously asked him about his views on the conservation of Botswana's wildlife heritage, he had been surprised to hear how Thopelo had reiterated many of the conservation sentiments that Mothinsi had expounded to him, during their memorable time together soon after his arrival in Maun. Charles had been most impressed how extremely well informed and up to date Thopelo had been.

'Charles, it is very much thanks to Botswana's stable government and progressive social policies that the country has emerged as one of Africa's bourgeoning biodiversity hotspots, and apart from minerals, ecotourism in Botswana is now one of our biggest sources of income.'

Like Mothinsi, Thopelo cited the founding of the Moremi Reserve as a huge step for Botswana. 'The country had increasingly focussed on wildlife conservation ever since the formation in the 1960s when the Batauana tribe established the Moremi Game Reserve in the Okavango Delta. And we can be proud of the fact that this was the first time the indigenous people had created such a wildlife sanctuary in Africa.'

'I met one of your fellow tribesmen who had a relative, Jack Ramsden, who had played a major role in the establishment of the Moremi Wildlife Reserve. Ramsden, together with a European couple called Robert and June Kay, was a founder member of the N'gamiland Conservation Society. They played a significant role in highlighting the plight of wildlife in the Okavango Delta, during the early part of the 1960s. It's a fascinating story.'

Thopelo was pleased to hear that a member of his Herero tribe had been so involved in the establishment of the Moremi Reserve. 'It was very much thanks to the stringent conservation measures that were established, and the subsequent abundance and diversity of wildlife to be found in this north-easterly region of Botswana, that the Okavango Delta soon earned the important status of being a UNESCO World Heritage Site. In recent years, our government has become increasingly aggressive in its efforts to stop poaching, with its anti-poaching laws being strictly enforced, largely by our highly trained military forces. Also, and perhaps most importantly, Botswana's wildlife conservation is largely left in the hands of local communities, which provides the local people with alternative revenue to that of poaching and wildlife trafficking. I've been told by a reliable governmental source that Botswana is soon to ban commercial hunting throughout the country altogether.'

*

The weeks leading up to Charles's departure from Nxau Nxau proved to be as hectic and dramatic as ever. Jefta had been arrested by the police and implicated in the murder of his niece, Esther Ochuros, and had been taken to a prison in Gumare to face trial. But as the police had been unable to discover the identity of any witchdoctor residing in a nearby village who might have cast the 'death spell' on Esther, they were now coming to the conclusion that either Jefta himself, or one of his criminal associates, had been responsible for her murder. Also, as Megano Angelo's name had been linked with that of Jefta's, a warrant had now been issued for his arrest.

'Capital punishment is still a legal penalty in Botswana, and the death sentence is usually issued upon cases of murder and is carried out by hanging,' Thopelo told Charles. 'However, what the police still have to establish is just who carried out the murder, and had it been a third party who had mutilated Esther's body who had subsequently placed her head under the chair of one of Jefta's arch enemies. No doubt you will be interested to know that the villager in question has been completely exonerated in not having been involved, in any way, in such an infamous crime.'

When leaving Nxau Nxau it had been Charles's intention to travel overland across the 'thirst-lands' of the desert to Namibia, and to follow the same route that Kgosi's ancestors had traversed in order to escape from the onslaught of General von Trotha's forces, at the beginning of the twentieth century. But, whilst in the process of organising this journey with a Greek trader whom Charles had met in Sehitwa, during his time camped on the shores of Lake Ngami, Tjipene delivered another note from Mothinsi.

The message read:

Prior to you departing to Namibia it is of the utmost importance for you to come back to Maun, and to accompany me to Gaberone where 'you know who' has told me that he considers it is essential for you to meet with him again. Please respond positively to this request, and please rest assured that you will be reimbursed for all of the additional expenses incurred.

As Charles felt he had no alternative but to agree to change his plans, soon after having received Mothinsi's message he handed another empty packet of cigarettes to Tjipene with a note, which read:

On my visit to Gumare this coming weekend I shall make a flight reservation on Air Botswana to fly to Maun, and as soon as I have purchased the ticket I shall let you know as to the flight's eta.

After having sent the note, Charles could not help thinking why Mr Colin Patterson, HM's Secretary of Economic Development at Gaberone's British High Commission, had now considered it so vital that they should see each other again.

During Charles's last weekend in Gumare, he had a most satisfactory meeting with Zhang at the Makgovango Luxury Inn, the place their first encounter had taken place just over three months ago, and Zhang had insisted that Charles should be his dinner guest. During their discussions, Zhang told Charles how thankful he had been for his introduction to Chief Tjamuaha, and to some of his elders, which had provided his Bazhong Hangheng Plc company the sole rights for mineral exploration throughout the lands that came under the chief's jurisdiction. And Zhang once more gave Charles his solemn word that the chief's Herero tribal people would be benefiting to the maximum should sizeable mineral deposits be found.

However, Zhang did not let on to Charles how he had purchased for his father three valuable minerals from Megano Angelo, and although he knew that as an ally of Jefta the police had issued an arrest warrant for him, he made no mention that Megano had recently left Gumare for good and had flown to Namibia. Also, he failed to inform Charles how he was planning to deceive his employees by falsifying some parts of the contract with the chief, to the ultimate benefit of his own bank account in Hong Kong.

After cabling Mothinsi the day and time of arrival in Maun, Charles collected a batch of mail from his box number at the post office which included not only letters from his parents, brother, school and university friends, but a most welcome letter from Christiane. Her scented handwritten letter had been mailed from her home address in Germany and had highlighted how much she had been missing him. Charles had been overjoyed to have such sentiments confirmed by her, for quite some time he had considered that with their months of separation their love for one another was now stronger than it had ever been, and he could not wait for their forthcoming planned meeting in Windhoek.

On the second-to-last night of Charles's stay in Nxau Nxau, Thopelo had been asked by Kgosi to arrange a farewell send-off for Charles, with Kisi having been delegated by him to arrange the party. This was to include tribal music, dancing and a feast of suckling pig, to be washed down no doubt with an abundant supply of the local beer, which had sorghum malt as its most important ingredient. Throughout Charles's time with the Herero tribal people, he had been fascinated by the variety of colourful dresses and hats that the womenfolk wore, particularly at their 'Born-Again Christian' celebrations, and other such festive and formal occasions.

'The way the Herero women dress had been heavily influenced by Western culture during the colonial period, for it incorporates and appropriates the styles of clothing worn by their German colonialists,' Thopelo had told him. 'And though the style was initially forced upon them, it now operates as a tradition and represents a point of pride. Herero women adopted the floor-length sombre-coloured gowns worn by German missionaries in the late nineteenth century, but now make them in far more vivid colours and prints. Married and older Herero women wear the dresses that are locally known as *ohorokova* every day, while younger and unmarried women wear them only on special occasions.'

When Charles had asked about what he considered to be the most distinctive feature of Herero women's dress, their horizontal horned headdress, Thopelo told him, 'These are known as *otjikaiva,* which is a symbol of respect, worn to pay homage to the cows that have historically sustained the Herero.

The headdresses can be formed from rolled-up newspaper covered in fabric and are made to match or to coordinate with dresses, and decorative brooches with pins attached to the centre fronts of the garment.'

A broad grin spread across Thopelo's wizened face. 'The overall intended effect is for the woman to resemble a plump, slow-moving cow and they often, which you may have noticed, when being photographed, are likely to adopt the "cow pose", with their arms raised and palms outstretched upwards.'

It appeared to Charles that a high percentage of the villagers had turned out to bid him farewell from their midst, their constant clapping and dancing being similar to what he had previously seen at one of their tribal weddings. The women were dressed in their most colourful of dresses, with some wearing the largest horizontally horned headdresses that he had ever seen. Kgosi and some of his closest elders, including Thopelo Riruako, were seated on chairs in a semi-circle in front of a group of potential dancers, bare-chested men and women in bras and shorts. All of whom were sitting cross-legged on the ground and maintaining a constant rhythmical clapping in unison to the footwork of the dancers who appeared to, in impromptu fashion, get up from the ground and energetically prance up and down in keeping with the clapping, and the beat of the drums in the background.

Much to Charles's surprise, the evening had ended with Chief Tjamuaha saying that he had an announcement to make.

'It is with much regret that we are soon to say goodbye to Charles Duncan here – it has been our pleasure to have an academic of his prowess with us in Nxau Nxau, who has shown such a keen interest in the history of our Herero tribe, as well as the traditions of our way of life. Therefore, I am taking this opportunity to wish him every future success in his further studies of our tribe, whilst he is with some of our forebears in our original homelands of Namibia. Also, in appreciation of the studies that he has carried out with us over the last few months, and the respect that he has shown to us all, it is my delight to appoint him as an honorary member of our Herero tribe here in Botswana.'

After which Kgosi presented Charles with a finely sculptured malachite figurine of a Herero woman dressed in her full Victorian costume, and a signed certificate to record the Herero honour that had been bestowed upon him. Many photographs were taken of the presentations.

All those in earshot of their chief burst into loud ululations and clapping, and after Kgosi and the elders had departed, the party continued into the early hours of the morning. Kisi and Charles were left on their own to enjoy their final time together, and reminisce over everything they had experienced from the night of Esther Ochuros's arrival in his hut, to all the drama surrounding her murder and the subsequent arrest of Jefta Kandorozu.

7

WESTWARD TO WINDHOEK

The Botswana Airlines flight from Maun arrived in Gaberone just after midday on the Saturday, and Mothinsi and Charles were met by a chauffeur who was holding a board with Mothinsi's name printed in large capitals upon it. After the driver had introduced himself, he led them to a black Mercedes, which had darkened one-way rear windows, parked in a restricted parking zone, and drove them to a bungalow on the outskirts of the city. And it was here that Colin Patterson had welcomed them to his home.

After a curry lunch that had been served to them by Patterson's house boy, they had been given coffee in the bungalow's spacious sitting room, which had its walls adorned by British hunting scenes, a portrait of HM the Queen on the wall above his desk, and an impressive view over an immaculately kept lawn with borders bursting with tropical colours.

'Charles, I very much appreciate you having agreed to change your plans in travelling to Namibia, and to go out of your way so we have this opportunity to meet again like this. But what you have managed to convey to us about the clandestine dealings of the two Herero tribesmen from Nxau Nxau with a Japanese gemstone dealer in Gumare, via Tjipene and Mothinsi here, has proved to be almost the tip of an iceberg with regards to many of the subversive activities that are currently taking place by both Japanese and Chinese operatives in Botswana. From the information that our High Commission is receiving, there has been a considerable increase of mineral corporations from both countries vying with each other as to how they can gain many of the exploration rights and thereby exploit the country's mineral wealth. An increasing number of these transactions have proved to be illegal and subsequently to the detriment of the tribal authorities concerned.'

Charles took a sip of his coffee. 'I already understood that to be the case. What was it that led to your decision that we should meet again?'

'An informer that we have managed to recruit from the Embassy of Japan here in Gaberone has recently told us that the Japanese gemstone dealer Katsuro Khama, whom you had made reference to in connection with his meetings in Gumare, has recently been found dead in his hotel room in the city. And according to the police he had either been murdered or had committed suicide. For a 4.5 pistol was found on the floor beside his body, the bullet had entered through the side of his forehead. The police, with the help of the Japanese embassy, are now carrying out a thorough investigation.'

Charles was shocked to hear about the untimely death of Katsuro Khama. 'I was always with my Chinese friend, Jinchu, on the few occasions that I had seen Katsuro with Jefta and Megano in a bar in Gumare. I was recently informed by Zhang Jinchu that Katsuro had left town and evidently, from various rumours that he had heard, had been in possession of the mineral sample that Jefta and Megano had given to him to value and to make an offer to purchase. However, from all subsequent reports, and in spite of the many enquiries that had been made, no one knew where Katsuro had disappeared to, and the last thing that we would have thought was that he was to either be murdered, or to have taken his own life.'

'After Katsuro Khama's death, the Japanese Embassy issued the following report: "Mr Khama came to Botswana just over a year ago as part of a Japanese delegation from Akita University, and was a well-respected expert in identifying mineral deposits. He initially worked with the university's research team in the study of geological conditions with the aim of determining the location of further mineral deposits in the country. As a result of these studies the Japanese government hoped that the Akita University research team of specialists will place it in a good position to, in future, acquire part of Botswana's natural resources in the midst of international conditions."'

Patterson paused, stood up and walked over to the window. 'Khama had left the Akita research team after only ten months of working for them, and had managed to successfully obtain from the Ministry of Minerals, Energy and Water Resources a licence to operate as an independent dealer in semi-precious mineral stones throughout Botswana. And since the granting of the licence, it is considered that he had dealings with what is rumoured to be a subversive Japanese trading company, Makoya Marubeni.'

Patterson turned around to look directly at Charles. 'How much do you know about your friend Zhang Jinchu? For the information that we have received is that his father is a senior gemstone specialist working for a major Chinese mineral corporation with its headquarters in Kitwe, Zambia. He has a reputation of being closely connected with his colleagues in actively negotiating mineral exploration rights from governments in both Central and Southern Africa. Did Zhang ever speak about his father and his many connections?'

'That information is totally new to me,' Charles replied. 'Zhang has never spoken about his father.'

'We have been informed that after the police had arrested Jefta Kandorozu for the murder of his niece, they are doing as much as possible to find the whereabouts of his close friend Megano Angelo, although they have received some unconfirmed reports that he has fled the country and is now in Namibia. Have you heard any reports to confirm this?' Charles could only reply that he had not.

'Those of us representing Western nations in Gaberone are becoming greatly concerned about the increased amount of conspiracies that are taking place in Botswana,' Patterson continued, 'and the number of clandestine dealings that unscrupulous mineral stone dealers from China and Japan are involved in. And in connection with some of the mineral rights that have been illegally negotiated by such operators, it appears that the conflict between the two countries is becoming more dangerous, which could have resulted in the reason for Katsuro Khama's untimely death.' Just before the house boy re-entered the room with a tray of tea, Patterson concluded, 'Charles, the chief reason for asking you here is to first congratulate you in having provided us with such invaluable information, and what we would like you to do is to continue in this way. However, this time to communicate with one of my colleagues in the British High Commission in Windhoek, and should you agree to this, I shall give you his name, but please do not write it down. Similarly, I will tell you the way that you can make contact with him. Also, in a recent note that I received in the diplomatic bag from Philip Eisenberg, he has asked me to pass on his appreciation for everything you have done on behalf of our intelligence-gathering in Botswana; he wishes you every success for your time in Namibia, and looks forward to seeing you again on your return to Durham in the autumn.'

Their conversation during the rest of the afternoon was taken up with the recent cricket news from home – particularly, as far as Charles was concerned, how Yorkshire was doing in the county championship. Also, just how Tony Blair's Labour government was handling the country's economy. On Charles's departure Mothinsi remained with Colin Patterson, no doubt for further confidential discussions, and on leaving Charles was given a fat envelope, which later he was to find contained a quantity of US and Namibian dollars, amounting to a sum of well over £500 sterling, and a priority Air Botswana ticket to Windhoek. After fond farewells and warm handshakes with Patterson and Mothinsi, he was driven to the Avani Hotel in Shuma Drive, where he was to stay the night prior to taking his flight to Windhoek the following morning.

Eating by himself in the hotel that evening, Charles could not help dwelling on the fact that Zhang had never made any mention of his father being an influential senior executive of a major mineral mining corporation operating in Southern Africa. He wondered just how much contact Zhang had had with his father during their observations of Jefta and Megano with Katsuro Khama, and the possible involvement of his father with Katsuro's subsequent death in Gaberone. Also, whether Zhang's father had in any way been involved with him in the drawing up of the mineral exploration rights contract that he had negotiated with Kgosi.

Charles was met at Windhoek's Hosea Kutako International Airport by a driver from Gaberone's British High Commission and driven to the nearby Windhoek Country Club, where Patterson had reserved a room for him. It was here that he met Patterson's diplomatic colleague, an extremely enthusiastic Mr Barrie Hicks. After the customary courtesy greetings, Hicks was quick to get down to business, and, similar to what Charles had been asked by Patterson to do when he had first arrived in Botswana, Hicks had said, 'Mr Duncan, as my colleague has no doubt already told you, our embassy here would also be most grateful if during your academic studies on the Herero tribe in this country, should you come across any evidence of foreign nationals negotiating for mineral exploration rights with the people you are with, or indeed hear rumours about such dealings, you would let me know.'

'As I said to Mr Patterson,' Charles replied, 'I am happy to do so as long as my studies of the Herero tribespeople are in no way jeopardised.'

'I can confirm that the source of any information that you are able to provide us with will be kept in the strictest of confidence, and I can give you my word that no one will ever be able to find out that you had been the source of the information concerned, for all such data would be in embassy code. Similar to Botswana, this country is currently experiencing an upsurge of illegal dealings being carried out by a number of infamous foreign mineral corporations, who appear to be vying with one another to secure as much of Namibia's vast mineral wealth as possible.'

Prior to Barrie Hicks' departure, he gave Charles a PO box number at Windhoek's general post office, located in a restricted area which was only available to the diplomatic embassies and High Commissions that were represented in the country, and to a few nominated associates that he was to be one of. He also reiterated, as Colin Patterson had previously told Charles, 'Although I would very much like to meet you again, regrettably, due to obvious security reasons, I shall most probably be unable to do so. And of course, similar to the practice established in Botswana, on no account must you try to make contact with me here at my office at the High Commission but rather, should anything be urgent and important, here is my secure personal number.'

Charles spent three days at the Country Club before travelling by train to Swakopmund, where he had decided to establish his base in Namibia. Swakopmund was just over 350 kilometres to the west of Windhoek and had been originally settled by German colonists in 1892. However, in Windhoek his first visit was to the National Archives of Namibia, which shared a building with Namibia's National Library, in which he was delighted to find that the archives held a complete collection of national newspapers from 1897 to 1962. In the climate-controlled archive building he was informed by its curator, Johan Erasmus, that it held in excess of 500,000 records, and some 800 history audio cassettes.

One of the history cassettes that Charles had time to listen to well outlined how the leadership of the Ovaherero is distributed over eight royal houses, with a Paramount Chief ruling over these eight traditional royal authorities, as well as how the Herero language (*Otjiherero*) represented the main unifying link among the Herero peoples. The cassette also made reference to the Herero religion being known as *Oupwee*, and highlighted how much the Herero people believed in *Okuruo* – holy fire – which represents an important link to their ancestors in order to speak to God and Jesus Christ on their behalf, and that the Herero are mostly Christians, primarily Roman Catholic, Lutheran and born-again Christians.

Due to the wealth of historical material held by the national archives and the museum, and the generous help and time that the curator had given him, Charles could well recognise that he would be returning to Windhoek in order to spend more time digging further into the literature which covered the background, characteristics and traditions of the Herero people. He was pleased to think how Christiane too would undoubtedly be spending much of her research activities in delving through the literature and invaluable photographic archives, in search of references to her ancestor, Duke Gustav von Braunschweig-Lüneberg.

As Charles had decided to establish his main base in Namibia at Swakopmund, when looking for suitable accommodation he had been attracted by the name of the Japie's Yard Wanderer's Inn, which had reasonably priced rooms and was only a short distance from the town centre. The inn was also in walking distance of the Sam Cohen Library, which he had been told by Johan (the curator of Windhoek library archives) also held an extensive collection of historical documents, photographs, postcards and over 10,000 books. And, similar to the Windhoek archives, the library contained newspapers from 1898 up to the present day. So, Charles knew that he would initially be spending a good deal of his research time at the Cohen Library to provide him with as good a background as possible on the social history and customs of the Herero tribe. He knew that Christiane would want to spend some time with him at Swakopmund and at the library too.

Swakopmund lies between the Namib Desert and the waves of the Atlantic Ocean. It sits at the '*mund*' (German for mouth) of the Swakop river; they named their new town accordingly. Now a city, it enjoys a desert climate with, on the whole, mild weather. Although the waters off Namibia's northern coast are notorious for their strong currents, and treacherous fog which has seen the demise of many ships, the city is protected from the Atlantic Ocean across its sandy beaches by an old sea wall, which is towered over by one of its most prominent landmarks, the 35m (115ft) lighthouse, which was built by the colonists in 1902. Its powerful light could be seen from as far as thirty-five nautical miles away.

Whilst exploring the city, where the streets were wide and lined with palm trees, Charles had found that many of the buildings represented fine examples of German architecture. These very much reminded him of similar buildings he had first seen when he had been on skiing holidays with his Durham University friends in Bavaria. Also, he had noted that some of the streets still carried the names of past colonial administrators. However, during Charles's first couple of weeks in Swakopmund he spent the majority of his time in the archival part of the Sam Cohen Library, and he could not have been more grateful to the library's Deputy Curator, a middle-aged softly spoken Herero scholar who asked Charles to just call him by his Christian name, Kakuii.

'I am in quite regular contact with Johan Erasmus in Windhoek and, like him, I could not be more delighted to help you in any way that I am able to in your research studies on the culture and traditions of my tribe,' he told Charles. 'Also, I shall be intrigued to hear about your findings whilst you were living for a few months in the Herero village of Nxau Nxau, which obviously must have been a great success, due to the chief of the village bestowing on you an honorary membership of the Herero tribal people of Botswana.'

The hundredth anniversary of the start of General Lothar von Trotha's genocide against the Herero and Nama people had fallen just before Charles's arrival in Namibia. On the anniversary a member of the German government, Heidemarie Wieczorek-Zeul, Germany's Minister for Economic Development and Cooperation, had officially apologised and expressed grief for the slaughter.

Members of General von Trotha's family had travelled to Omarurus, by invitation of the Herero chiefs, and publicly apologised for the actions of their relative. Wolf-Thilo von Trotha stated, 'We, the von Trotha family, are deeply ashamed of the terrible events that took place one hundred years ago. Human rights were grossly abused at that time.'

At the time of these two occasions, people had been reminded how in 1904, General von Trotha had declared in the German press, 'Hereros are no longer German citizens, and no war may be considered humanely against non-humans.' And how, at the same time, the general had issued his infamous Extermination Order (*'Vernichtungsbefehl'*) that had, between the years 1904–1907, accounted for an estimated 75,000 indigenous people being killed.

The last letter that Charles had received from Christiane in mid-July had been full of her enthusiasm that within the next week she would be flying to Namibia and that they would be in each other's company again. In previous communications they had arranged to meet soon after her arrival in Windhoek, hire a car and spend the next ten days together travelling to northern Namibia and visiting the Etosha National Park, travelling to the west through parts of the Skeleton Coast National Park and then down south to Swakopmund. His parents had also written to say how delighted they had been to see that he had been made an honorary member of the Herero tribe, and had thanked him for the photographs of the award ceremony that he had sent them.

However, just prior to their reunion, Charles received in his personal PO box an envelope which contained a Botswana police service report to record that the Japanese licensed precious stone dealer Katsuro Khama had been murdered, and that it was now considered that he had not committed suicide. For the police had found in his belongings a note that had threatened Katsuro's life if he was to continue his investigations in Maun, where he had last examined the gemstone, into the identity of who had taken it from him.

The police report recorded how the 4.5 revolver had been found on the floor to the left of Katsuro's body, with the bullet hole having penetrated the left side of his skull. However, his girlfriend had informed the police that Katsuro was right-handed and would never have picked anything up with his left hand. She had also reported that during the few days leading up to his death, he had received a number of anonymous phone calls, which appeared to have made him increasingly concerned. The report concluded that the police, with the assistance of the Japanese Embassy, were doing as much as possible to search for the murderer(s) of Mr Katsuro Khama, and to have him or them brought to justice at the earliest opportunity.

After reading the police report, Charles could only reflect on his times with Zhang watching some of Katsuro's meetings with Jefta and Megano in Gumare. And as he considered that there may be a possibility that Zhang could know something more about Katsuro's business connections, he decided to mail a copy of the police report to him. In a covering note he wrote that should he have any information that he considered could be of interest to the police in their search for the murderer, to get into contact with them in Gaberone, direct. For Charles had always considered that Zhang had known a good deal more about Katsuro that he had let him know.

Christiane looked as radiant as ever when Charles went to meet her at the guesthouse, which her German Embassy had placed at her disposal during her time in Namibia. Such was the influence of her von Braunschweig-Lüneberg ancestry, and her great-grandfather's reputation whilst serving as a senior representative of the German government's Ministry of Foreign Affairs, during the latter part of the nineteenth and early twentieth century. Also, much to her delight, she had been given the use of one of the embassy's BMW 4x4 vehicles, which had saved Charles having to hire a car.

Prior to driving just over 400 kilometres north to the Etosha National Park, they spent their first night together at the Windhoek Country Club. Charles had booked two single rooms for them, although when an African porter had carried their bags to the adjoining rooms he had obligingly, perhaps expecting a larger gratuity than was customary, and to the amusement of them both, rather dramatically produced a key and unlocked the connecting door between the two bedrooms.

Although keeping to the pact that Christiane had insisted upon, that out of wedlock she would never be willing to fully consummate their relationship, Charles felt he had been wafted into heaven in having her in his arms again. Just after the sun's rays had started to filter through the curtains of their bedroom on the following morning, Charles decided to tell Christiane everything that had happened to him in Nxau Nxau. This had included the ramifications of the murder of Esther Ochuros, and his initial contact with her in the tribal guesthouse.

Christiane had initially giggled when Charles had told her that soon after his arrival in the village, a young African maiden had entered his bed, and how when he had felt her body making contact with his, he had thought that he was dreaming about being with her when they first slept together at his family's home at Hartlington Hall. But when Charles had continued to tell her about her subsequent murder and the witchcraft conspiracy that had evolved, she gave him another hug, and left their bed to make herself a strong coffee.

During the rest of their first day together, before setting off to the Etosha National Park on the following morning, they spent the majority of their time telling each other as much as possible about their lives since they had been parted. Although Charles decided not to tell Christiane the details of the way that Esther had been murdered, or to mention anything about the precious gemstone that Katsuro Khama had taken from Jefta Kandorozu, and his subsequent murder in Gaberone. But he did tell her as much as possible about the traditions and culture of the Herero tribe, and how proud he had been when on his final night at Nxau Nxau, Chief Tjamuaha had made him an honorary member. And, in all probability due to this honour, how already he had been so well received by the curator of Namibia's National Museum in Windhoek, as well as by the Scientific Society and the deputy Herero curator of the Sam Cohen Library.

During their five-hour drive north up to the Etosha National Park they decided not to talk too much about the past, but rather just to relax and to enjoy each other's company during the adventure ahead of them. They had decided that when they had made their booking at the Namutoni Fort rest-camp at the edge of Etosha Pan in the Oshikoto region of northern Namibia, they would just book a double room, not to have the unnecessary expense of having to pay for two. Christiane had jokingly said,

'After all, as our relationship hasn't been consummated, there isn't anything illegal about us sharing a bed together.' Also, she knew that after her arrival in the country, her parents would not know her whereabouts in order to check on such matters, other than having her address and contact number at her accommodation in Windhoek.

The Namutoni Fort was in a vast, sandy plain and was one of the entrance gates to the Etosha National Park. The fort's brilliantly whitewashed walls represented a striking contrast to the sandy environment in which it so dominantly stood. After a long and dusty journey up to the fort, and with the temperature hovering at around 20°C, they had been pleased to have enjoyed taking a shower, prior to having tea under the shade of a clump of palm trees in the fort's forecourt with some newly arrived other campers. After tea, a smartly dressed member of the local Ovambo tribe took them all on a guided tour of the fort and its perimeter.

The guide, who told the small gathering to call him Oshi, proved to have a good command of both the English and German languages apart from his native Ovambo. Oshi started his tour by telling them that the first construction of a fort on the sight had been carried out by the German colonists in 1896, first used as a police post, then as a veterinary control post, before being used during the First World War to hold British prisoners of war. Then, after walking to the fort's main gate, he showed them an old bronze plaque to record the names of seven brave German men who, in January 1904, had managed to successfully repulse the attack on the fort by hundreds of Ovambo tribesmen. This had been mainly due to the Ovambo only having been partly armed with the almost obsolete Martini-Henry single-loaded rifles, against the colonists' more rapid-fire ones.

After this, Oshi had taken them a short distance from the entrance to show them a more modern plaque, commemorating the many equally brave Ovambo warriors who had been killed, whos casualties were estimated at sixty-eight dead, forty missing and twenty wounded. Oshi told them, 'In recognition of the Namutoni Fort's military past, it is our tradition to herald in sunrise and sunset by a bugle call, which is performed by an ex-Namibian policeman from the watchtower at the north-eastern corner of the fort.' He added, 'The latter call will be the sign for us all to enjoy "sundowners" in the courtyard.'

While having a *briface* around a campfire in the main courtyard that evening, Oshi told them, 'The night before my tribal ancestors attacked the fort, the seven German occupants had had an extensive, rich, heavy dinner, which was customary for the colonists to celebrate Kaiser Wilhelm II's birthday. They had all felt rather hungover when the attack had taken place.' He then joked, 'However, please rest assured that no matter how much you eat or drink this evening, I shall guarantee that the fort will not be under any type of siege after the bugle call at sunrise tomorrow morning.'

Later on in the evening when Charles and Christiane had been left by the themselves and were relaxing by the smouldering embers of the campfire, they fell into a discussion about some of the terrible incidents that had taken place at the beginning of the twentieth century in German South West Africa. For after all, it was the main reason for her visit to Namibia to see whether or not one of her ancestors had been involved with the genocide that had taken place.

'Christiane, from what I have read about the Ovambo attack that took place here at the Namutoni Fort it was of course a minor incident in comparison to the slaughter that occurred after the tribal uprisings that took place against their colonial masters. Between 1904 and 1907, an estimated eighty per cent of the Herero tribe died during the war, many from starvation as they had been driven into the desert, an environment not too dissimilar to what we have driven through today.'

'Yes it was a relatively minor incident, but it's awful to think that in this very place there were so many needless deaths. I know that during my studies I will be faced with a great many uncomfortable truths, very possibly about my own ancestor, but I need to find out all I can.'

Charles replied, 'Sometimes the truth can be extremely hurtful, but I am sure that during your time here in Namibia you will be able to establish how much your ancestor, if at all, was involved in such awful atrocities.'

On returning to their small room in the fort, which could well have been a converted cell from the time it was being used to accommodate First World War British prisoners of war, they soon fell into bed. They had agreed to try to blank out from their minds the atrocities they had been discussing. But rather, Charles told Christiane how very much he had been missing her, and how much he loved her. While they both continued with such mutual romantic explicits, and whilst still mumbling to each other, they fell asleep, no doubt enjoying blissful dreams of their future together. The next thing that they became aware of was to be woken from their embrace by the fort's bugle call at sunrise.

Their two days visiting the Etosha National Park proved to be above their expectations. After a sundowner at the Etosha Pan's Okaukuejo camp they were able to see for their first time the notoriously shy and endangered black rhinoceros, which had been strolling slowly down to drink from one of the nearby floodlit water holes. In spite of the disastrous poaching and needless bloodshed of black rhinos throughout Southern Africa's national parks, which had made it one of the continent's most endangered species, so far the Etosha National Park had been almost unaffected by the onslaught of poaching. Namibia could boast the largest population of black rhinoceroses in the world, most of which were in the vast expanses of the park.

It took them just over three days to drive from Etosha through parts of the Skeleton Coast National Park to Swakopmund. Charles told Christiane that the indigenous Sand people referred to the Skeleton Coast as 'The Land God Made in Anger', and that it was reputed to be one of the most remote wilderness areas in Africa. However, they both had found the wide desert plains and dry river valleys, with some spectacular rock formations where huge chunks of strata-striped rock lay twisted and eroded in the riverbeds, to be an environment that neither had ever previously seen the likes of before. They stayed the nights at small campsites in what seemed to them to be as near to 'Mother Nature' as possible. And, more often than not, being awoken at sunrise by troops of baboons heralding the daylight by barking at each other from nearby boulder-strewn *kopjes*.

As they drove along the sandy, gravel-like roadways, they had been overjoyed in seeing herds of elephants, giraffes, zebra, gemsbok, impala and ostriches, that had all successively adapted to living in such a desert-like stony environment. It had been the first time that Charles and Christiane had experienced, when gazing across a vast expanse of sand, the sensation of seeing a 'mirage', for they both insisted that they could see a vast lake on the horizon.

As the temperature had risen to the around 25°C, they had made sure to carry as much water with them as possible, which included hanging the customary canvas bag of water in front of their vehicle's radiator. However, during their trip through the Skeleton National Park, one of their most memorable occasions was just after the first rays of the sun had started to cast their shadows between the vast windswept, sculptured hillocks of sand dunes. They struggled up the spine to the top of one of the highest of them and then, by digging their heels into the side of the mountain of sand, raced one another to the foot of the sand dune, and then collapsed in each other's arms, laughing and exhausted.

After leaving the heated sands of the Namib Desert it was quite a relief for them to arrive at Swakopmund and to rejoice in being refreshed by the breeze wafting over them from the

Atlantic Ocean. Charles had decided that it would be more sensible not to have Christiane staying with him at Japie's Yard Wanderer's Inn, but rather he had reserved a double room at Hotel A La Mer, which overlooked the old town's impressive coastline.

Although Charles had returned to his base at Wanderer's Inn on several occasions, he had informed the proprietor, Dolf Labuschagne, that for the next week or so he would be 'coming and going'. But, during the daytime, Christiane and he spent the majority of their time in connection with their respective studies at the Sam Cohen Library, and being greatly assisted by Kakuii the Deputy Curator. In the evenings they spent their time together at the Hotel A La Mer, often walking prior to dinner by the old sea wall, and to any onlooker they appeared very much as if they were just a young, happy, married couple.

8

AN UNEXPECTED SIGHTING

After Christiane had spent ten days with Charles in Swakopmund, just before her planned return to her base in Windhoek at the end of August the main ceremony of the Herero's special day was due to take place at Okahandja, in Central Namibia. As Christiane had been particularly interested in attending these celebrations, they had decided to visit Okahandja on her way back to Windhoek. As Kakuii had been born and brought up in Okahandja, he had expressed great interest in accompanying them and had been of such help to them during their research work at the Sam Cohen Library, they agreed to take him with them. They fully recognised that it would be of considerable advantage to them to be accompanied by a person who could speak the Herero Bantu language, *Otjiherero*.

Christiane had read about this annual celebration in the German language newspapers stored at the library, and how it was in honour of the day and the place that Herero chief Samuel Maharero's body was buried in 1923, alongside his ancestors in Okahandja. She noted that it had been Chief Maharero who had in January 1904 led the uprising of the Herero against the colonists, which had resulted in the slaughter of 123 Europeans in Okahandja. There was a reference to her great-grandfather, Duke Gustav von Braunschweig-Lüneberg, when serving as the senior representative of Foreign Affairs in the German colony, being quoted as stating that following the Herero's subsequent defeat on the 11 August 1904 at the Battle of Waterberg, Chief Samuel Maharero had managed to escape to the Bechuanaland Protectorate.

This had been Christiane's opportunity to add some additional data to Charles's documentation. 'Whereas, as you already know, an estimated four to six thousand Herero warriors had fled into the Kalahari Desert, only just over a thousand managed to reach the British-administered Bechuanaland Protectorate,' she told him. 'But, unlike the other Herero refugees who had managed to gain asylum there, in 1907 the chief decided to move to the Transvaal in South Africa. And sixteen years later, on 14 March 1923, he died, and in the August of that year his body was transferred to the burial site of his ancestors in Okahandja, where he was reburied.'

'I'm surprised the government allowed it at that time,' Charles said. 'They must have considered how important this would be to the Herero people.'

'Evidently, the South African government was unaware of the role this event to commemorate their deceased forefathers would play as a commemoration of anti-colonisation and a symbol of nationalism, and therefore granted permission for the chief's reburial,' Christiane continued. 'According to the accounts, the annual three-day gathering starts with a procession to several graves of Herero chiefs, followed by a church service, with the men wearing military-style uniforms, and the women being in their traditional colourful dresses with voluminous skirts of many layers, their heads adorned by their traditional cow-horn pointed hats.'

'There's an annual holiday to commemorate the reburial of Chief Maharero called Namibia's Heroes' Day, also known as Red Flag Heroes' Day, and by the UN as Namibian Day, celebrated annually on 25 August,' Charles added. 'It's also a national holiday to commemorate those who died during the Namibian War of Independence, which began on 26 August 1966. SWAPO, the political independence party, with its People's Liberation Army, had deliberately chosen the date of their first armed struggle, and for the day to represent a symbol of nationalism and to highlight the strength and pride of the country's indigenous people and their respect for their deceased chieftains and ancestors.'

Their shared research was progressing well; Christiane could contribute information from the many German language resources that Charles would not otherwise have access to. They inspired each other to spend time gathering as much information as they could.

Before leaving Swakopmund, Charles was well aware that once Christiane had returned to the flat that had been provided for her by the German Embassy in Windhoek, it would be *verboten* for her to have him as her guest in her one-bedroom accommodation. So, they had decided that as Windhoek was only seventy kilometres north of Okahandja, she would drive back to the capital by herself, whereas Kakuii and he would return to Swakopmund by train. They would be with each other again at the Windhoek Country Club whilst they were completing their respective studies, before returning to Europe.

It took them just over five hours to drive to Okahandja, and to arrive at the Sylvanette Guest House, where Charles had booked two rooms. On the journey Kakuii had provided them with a considerable amount of additional valuable information.

The settlement was founded by the Herero and Nama tribes around 1800 but in 1850, the historical animosity between the two tribes resulted in the Battle of Moordkoppie, the Afrikaans word for Murder Hill.'

'Kakuii, one of the history books that you gave me said that in 1894 the governor of the German colony, Theodor Leutwein, whom my ancestor served under, had established an important military post in the town,' said Christiane. 'So, I would be most interested to see whether there is any monument to Leutwein in the city, and if there are any reports of my great-grandfather having ever visited Okahandja.'

'I know the person at the City Hall responsible for looking after such historical matters, and I shall arrange for you to have a meeting with him,' Kakuii replied. 'One monument that it is important for you to see is the Heroes Cemetery, where our two most significant Herero chiefs, Tjamuaha Maharero and Samuel Maharero, are buried. There are many other gravestones of our ancestors who were killed in battles with both the Nama and the German colonists. Similarly, perhaps we should take part in the service of thanksgiving at the Rhenish Mission Church, which was built in the sign of a cross in 1876 – not only the oldest construction in Okahandja, but the oldest building in Namibia. We should also visit the German fort that Theodor Leutwein had constructed.' So, Charles and Christiane agreed that during their time together in Okahandja, they would be happy to follow his lead to the most appropriate places for them to visit.

Whilst Kakuii had been talking about the number of Herero and Nama that had been killed, either in tribal warfare or by tribal uprisings against German colonial power, he touched on the atrocities that had taken place at the Shark Island concentration camp in Lüderitz Bay, Central Namibia.

'Charles, I know that you have already read a great deal about this concentration camp, but an internal report, initially published by the German Imperial Colonial Office, that has only just come to light, records that an estimated almost eight thousand Herero and two thousand Nama died in the various camps that the Germans had established in their colony.

Apparently a significant proportion of these, about three thousand, lost their lives on Shark Island.'

The Sylvanette Guest House turned out to be most conveniently placed in the heart of Okahandja. They spent their first evening enjoying sundowners sitting in the sheltered patio near to a small swimming pool, listening to Kakuii telling them more about the history of the tribal rivalry that still goes on between his Herero tribe and the Nama people. 'Regrettably, more often than not these skirmishes are more likely to take place on the anniversary of the 1850 Battle of Moordkoppie, but we may still see a few disturbances tomorrow on Heroes' Day.'

The 25 August turned out to be a most informative time for Charles and Christiane, and Kakuii proved to be a great asset, as he managed to enthusiastically guide them to all of the most important venues throughout Okahandja's Herero festivities. Kakuii had taken photographs of them in front of the monument to the two most famous of his Herero chiefs, Tjamuaha and Samuel Maharero, and told them, 'The fire over there is known as the Okuruo, a holy fire that during the festivities will never be allowed to burn out, for this is the way the chiefs and fellow Hereros establish contact with their ancestors.'

As they had joined the processions to several graves of Herero chiefs, Christiane, so impressed with what she was seeing, said to Kakuii, 'I can understand why the Herero women are so admired for their beauty and style; they look so elegant – and this is the first time I've seen this traditional dress – these long skirts really show the graceful way they walk. Many European women would be very envious!'

That evening, they were having a meal at the Amaegoesab Bar and Grill when Charles spotted an African man in the corner who seemed familiar. He was with another African and two Chinese men. After having excused himself from Christiane and Kakuii, he managed to edge his way through the crowded bar to get a better look, and just before he sat down with the three others, sitting with his back to him, he had been astonished to have recognised Megano Angelo.

Charles quickly returned to the company of Christiane and Kakuii, and said, 'Kakuii, I have not told you about some of the incidents that happened whilst I was carrying out my studies and living at Nxau Nxau. While I was there, a young Herero teenage girl was murdered – the Botswana police consider this was due to a witchdoctor's curse as she possibly knew the whereabouts of a valuable mineral deposit site close to the village. She knew the names of the two village elders who were involved in the clandestine selling of valuable gemstones to a Japanese gem dealer. Just before her murder she was about to let her village chief know all about the mineral deposit, as well as name the two tribal elders who were attempting to deceive and swindle him.'

Kakuii was visibly shocked. 'The poor girl, a victim of corruption. Did the police find the killers?'

'One of the two elders concerned, Jefta Kandorozu, has subsequently been charged with the murder of the teenager. Whereas the police have issued an order for the arrest of his fellow conspirator, Megano Angelo, who had with Jefta attempted to sell a valuable uncut diamond from the Nxau Nxau site, but he was known to have fled the country after Jefta's arrest. Kakuii, the reason for telling you all this is that Megano Angelo is sitting at a table in the corner over there, with his back to us, with another African and two Chinese gentlemen.'

'As you already know I was born in Okahandja and have many friends here – one of these is a superintendent in the Namibian Police Force, also known as Nampol, and is serving as a senior officer in the forces Crime Investigation Directorate,' Kakuii responded. 'So, if you will excuse me, I shall make contact with my friend who I know will be greatly interested in you having recognised the person concerned. I feel sure that the superintendent will be quick to organise a plan of action. But in the meantime, please keep an eye on their table, and I shall be back with you as soon as possible.'

By the time Kakuii had returned, Megano was still deep in conversation with the two Chinese men, with the latter taking notes on what he had been telling them. 'My superintendent friend was most grateful to receive the information that you had recognised a fugitive from Botswana. And he has returned here with me with two of his plain-clothes detectives, I have pointed out the man in question to them, and he has assured me that he has placed a "tail" on the man, to track him to wherever he goes. They will know where he is, and with whom he is associating. However, before arresting Megano and sending him back to Botswana to face criminal charges, the police are anxious to establish whether he is already involved in any clandestine dealings in Namibia.'

'It's such a coincidence that he should happen to be here in the same place as us tonight,' said Christiane. 'How fortunate you have a friend in the police that can take action so quickly.'

'Similar to the Botswana government, our government is becoming increasingly concerned about the number of illegal deals that are being carried out by Chinese and Japanese companies in their desire to dominate access to the country's wealth of mineral resources. Recently, a number of other countries, including Canada and Russia, have been keen to increase their facilities for nuclear power as an alternative to fossil fuels, which has given rise to their increased demand for uranium.'

By the time they had left the Amaegoesab Bar, Megano was still sitting at the table with the three others, and Charles was pleased that he had his back to where they had been sitting so he had not had the opportunity to possibly recognise him. He had now every confidence that the whereabouts of Jefta Kandorozu's criminal accomplice would be carefully monitored, in order to establish whether Megano had already embarked on illicit dealings in minerals with some fraudulent governmental officials or corrupt tribal elders.

Soon after this unexpected sighting of Megano Angelo, Charles decided at this stage not to inform Colin Patterson in Botswana, via Barrie Hicks at Windhoek's British High Commission, until he had discussed the matter further with Kakuii. He needed to know how long Kakuii's police superintendent friend required before having Megano arrested and returned to face trial in Botswana. Charles knew that this was unlikely to be until the latter part of his time at his base in Swakopmund. He did not wish to put anything in the way of the Namibian's police monitoring of Megano's meetings. However, Charles had vowed to himself, whether or not Megano was found to be acting illegally in Namibia, that if, at the trial of Jefta Kandorozu, it was established that Megano had been connected with the murder of Esther Ochuros, he would ensure that Megano would be returned to Botswana to face trial for her gruesome murder.

The following couple of days were spent visiting Leutwein's German fort, the library and the archives at the city hall. At the latter, Kakuii had introduced Christiane to his old university friend Ulrich Freidrich, of German/Herero descent. Ulrich had managed to locate one incidence of Christiane's ancestor having visited Okahandja in 1903, the year prior to the Herero and Nama uprising against their German colonial overlords. The record read:

Okahandja was honoured to have an official visit of Prince von Braunschweig-Lüneberg of the German Imperial Government's Ministry of Foreign Affairs. The Duke, on behalf of his Excellency, Theodor Leutwein, Colonial Administrator of German South West Africa, inspected a Guard of Honour at the German Fort, which was celebrated with a fanfare by the garrison's fine military band.

'During Leutwein's ten-year appointment as the country's Colonial Administrator his personal goal had been to create "colonialism without bloodshed",' Ulrich told them. 'And during his tenure he adopted what he referred to as the "Leutwein system", which represented a mixture of diplomacy, "divide-and-rule" and military force. Although his relationships with the indigenous tribes, including our Herero tribe, were tenuous at best.

'However, Leutwein was often criticised by fellow German colonists as being too lenient with us indigenous people, but in spite of that, at the start of the tribal uprising in 1904, Leutwein admitted that the Germans had not taken one Herero prisoner. Because of this Kaiser Wilhelm II replaced Leutwein with the notorious General Lothar von Trotha, which gave rise to the horrors of the bloodshed that followed.'

Christiane thanked Ulrich for the information that he had gathered on her behalf, and said, 'I have now been able to find out that when Theodor Leutwein left the country, my ancestor went back to Germany with him, and was never to return to South West Africa. Also, according to one press report, my ancestor was a great supporter of Leutwein's strategy of "colonialism without bloodshed", and had been quoted as saying that he totally refuted the military tactics adopted by General von Trotha with his "annihilation order" against the Herero and Nama people, recording that, "Every Herero will be shot on sight." On my ancestor's return to Germany, he did everything possible to support the Chancellor, Bernhard von Bülow, and his government in putting pressure on Kaiser Wilhelm II to replace von Trotha from his command, which, most regrettably, the emperor did too late to prevent further bloodshed.'

Ulrich said how glad he was to hear about the stance that Christiane's great-grandfather had adopted, and added, 'Prior to the tribal uprising in 1904 the Herero population was estimated at around 80,000, whereas in the 1911 census, only 15,000

Hereros were recorded as living in German South West Africa. Currently, there are over 200,000 Herero living in Namibia, which constitutes approximately seven per cent of the country's total population – a similar percentage to that of the Europeans living here.'

On the morning of their departure from Okahandja, Christiane had driven them to the station, which Kakuii told them had been built by the Germans in 1902 in order to provide a rail track from Windhoek to what was then their only access to a seaport at Swakopmund. Before a rather tearful goodbye, prior to Christiane driving herself the seventy kilometres or so back to her base in Windhoek, Charles promised that as soon as he had finished his studies in Swakopmund he would come up to stay at the Country Club to complete his research in the archives of Windhoek's National Museum.

'This will certainly be in less than three weeks' time,' he said, 'so I shall just catch you before your return to Europe, and mine to England about a fortnight later.'

After a final hug, Charles joined Kakuii with their bags in a surprisingly clean carriage and was grateful to have a travelling companion with him. For during their return to Swakopmund, Kakuii managed to take his mind away from just thinking about his future with Christiane, by providing him with some further much-valued information about the country's historical, and perhaps current, involvement with witchcraft.

'*Omuroi* is a Herero noun for someone suspected of practising witchcraft. A person who can fly at night, or rides on people at night, and who, in people's minds, resembles a ghost person or is like a phantom. Some people struggle to sleep when a certain person is around, due to their belief that the person possesses *omeros*. Others claim that such beings talk to them at night, and that when voices are heard, shouting at them can scare them away, or that sleeping with a candle by their beds helps, as omeros are adverse to light. These traditions are passed down from one generation to another and are still current in modern Herero culture,' Kakuii explained. 'As I mentioned to you both at Okahandja, Herero people believe in Okuruo (holy fire) which represents an important link for them to their ancestors, and to speak to God and Jesus Christ on their behalf. For although the Herero are mostly Christians, they still consider that it is important to retain this holy-fire link with their forefathers.'

On the train's late afternoon arrival in Swakopmund, Kakuii thanked Charles greatly for having hosted his time with them at the Heroes' Day weekend festivities, told him how he looked forward to helping further with his research programme at the library, and said, 'In the meantime, I want to try to arrange a meeting for you with one of our local Herero chiefs who, regrettably, due to his old age was unable to come to this year's Heroes' Day celebration. But the chief in question is a mine of knowledge about the traditions and customs of our tribe, and I know that he would be most interested in meeting you, particularly to hear about your studies in Botswana.' Charles had responded to this suggestion with enthusiasm.

The day after Charles's return to Swakopmund, he managed to make contact with Christiane. 'During our time away together, as my parents had been unable to make contact with me in Windhoek they had phoned the German Embassy to ask them to find out where I was, for they feared something may have happened to me. Although I had mentioned to the Under Secretary of the Embassy, who had showed me my accommodation and had given me the keys to the vehicle, that I was to start my research in Swakopmund, he had not relayed this information to the embassy itself. However, I did tell him that as I had kindly been given the loan of an embassy car, I would be taking the opportunity to do some sightseeing on my way to Swakopmund, and hoped to meet up with one of my Durham University friends, who is also undertaking a research project here in Namibia.'

'It's quite understandable that your parents were worried. Did you manage to speak to them?'

'This morning, I was able to use a phone at the embassy and spoke to my father who, after he had given me a good ticking-off for not having told them that I was going to be away from my base at Windhoek, he did eventually soften the tone of his voice to tell me how relieved he now was to hear that I was safe and sound. However, I obviously didn't mention to him that I had been away on holiday with you – my parents would have been shocked to hear that their daughter had been away with a man, and co-inhabiting with you or, for that matter, with any other person!'

Charles had now just under three more weeks based in Swakopmund, before returning to Windhoek to make some final checks at the National Archives on all of the data that he had managed to gather about the Herero tribe, during his three-month stay in Namibia. Kakuii did everything he could to provide him with as much information as possible about the culture and traditions of his fellow tribal people.

Chief Hosea Riruko, who was in his mid-eighties, had handed over the day to-day running of his responsibilities to his eldest son, and lived in the small settlement of Arandis, to the north-east of Swakopmund. His quite sizeable house had an impressive peaked thatched roof with a rectangular doorway, surrounded by the ubiquitous poultry pecking around in the sandy surroundings and a number of the customary barking dogs. Charles had found that the houses in Nxau Nxau had much higher peaks to the thatch-work, some of which were plumbed by sizeable real cow horns, similar to those sculpted as the dominating feature of the headgear worn by Herero women.

Prior to meeting Chief Riruko, Kakuii had told Charles that the chief had, during the mid-1960s, been imprisoned for a while by Namibia's South African Administrators for his support and involvement with SWAPO's People's Liberation Army during the Namibian War of Independence, and due to this had been a highly respected Herero chieftain. In spite of his age, the chief had turned out to have retained an encyclopaedic knowledge of the history of his tribesmen and was most interested to hear from Kakuii that Charles had been made an honorary member of the Herero. The ageing chief showed great interest in Charles's studies on whether the culture and traditions of his Herero cousins in Botswana contrasted significantly to those of his ancestors, who had managed to survive the massacres at the beginning of the twentieth century.

After Kakuii had introduced Charles to Chief Riruko, they were served a dish of *Omarere*, the basis of the Herero diet, a sour milk product usually stored in large calabashes which each evening are topped up with fresh milk. Later, he told Christiane, 'I had to struggle through what I was presented with more out of politeness than by choice, as it was awful!'

Close to the chief's residence was a large enclosure, which was fenced off with wooden stakes in order to keep his animals confined and safe from nocturnal predators, and the enclosure also provided the animals with a sizeable thatched sheltered area. During Charles's discussions, the chief told him, 'Similar to my Herero cousins in Botswana, cattle still form the centre of our lives, and individual values have always been a measure of our individual tribal wealth.'

Charles told the chief as much as possible about his findings. 'I have been particularly impressed to find that the majority of the traditions and cultures of the Herero descendants in Botswana of those who managed to flee during the massacres have been successfully handed down to them by their forefathers. Because of these tribal teachings from one generation to another, I have established that there is very little difference to be found in the values that your tribes have maintained here in Namibia, and those of your Herero cousins now having lived for several generations in Botswana.'

The chief smiled. 'That is reassuring, Charles. I had very much hoped to hear that would be the case.'

'Setting aside the similarity of your ancestral inherited tribal values, the major contrast between the two groups of Hereros is the way that the womenfolk here in Namibia have adopted the Victorian-style dresses of the German colonists and the men, on special occasions, wearing the military-like fantasy uniforms. I have also been struck that some of the architecture here is so similar to that of a town in Bavaria, Romanesque and Gothic-inspired, high ceilings and columns.'

'Our colonial heritage,' the chief replied. 'We have little to thank the colonists for, but the architecture is certainly a feature of our town.'

Charles said, 'I found one of the finest examples of German architecture in Swakopmund to be the building known as the *Prinzessin Rupprecht Heim,* which I was told was built by the Germans in 1902 as a military hospital, and had been named after the wife of the Crown Prince of Bavaria. Also, when I visited a part of the museum, I was fascinated to see an exact replica of an early twentieth-century German chemist shop. For this had a fine comprehensive collection of pharmaceutical items being available to the citizens of Swakopmund at the time of its operation.'

'In those days, in the early part of the last century, in all probability it is unlikely that the indigenous people would either be able to afford, or perhaps not even be allowed, to enter such a European-owned premises,' said the chief. 'And even if they had been instructed to collect some medicine for their German masters, they would have had to receive it from a separate back entrance. This hardly improved when South Africa took over the administration of our country after the First World War, until Namibia gained its independence in March 1990.'

After their morning meeting with Chief Riruko, Kakuii was driving Charles further north, to Cape Cross. He had been lent one of the Scientific Society of Swakopmund's 4x4 vehicles for the day to take Charles to meet the chief, and had also been given permission to drive Charles to this part of the Namib Desert's shoreline with the Atlantic Ocean, where a spectacular colony of Cape fur seals could be seen, an estimated population of between 100,000 and 250,000.

Mothinsi had told Charles about the colony when they had been together in Maun, on hearing that Charles was going to spend some time in Swakopmund. 'Charles, with my considerable interest in natural history, I have read a great deal about the abundance of wildlife that can be seen in the area of Namibia that you are planning to visit. So, apart from your studies on my Herero tribal cousins, it is important for you to travel north from Swakopmund, up the coast through a part of the Namib Desert to Cape Cross, where you will be able to see one of the largest colonies of Cape fur seals in the world.

'Perhaps even more importantly you should take a trip to the south of Swakopmund to Walvis Bay. I have read that from there, you will be able to see not only more colonies of fur seals, but also a profusion of birdlife on a nearby huge natural lagoon where large flocks of pelicans and flamingos gather. And from Walvis Bay you can hire a kayak and paddle to Pelican Point – there is every chance you will see the two species of dolphins which are evidently abundant in this region of the Atlantic Ocean.' Mothinsi had added rather wistfully, 'And how I wish I was able to accompany you on such a spectacular natural history adventure.'

During Charles's last weeks in Swakopmund, Kakuii had once more gained permission for the loan of the Scientific Society's vehicle, and they had been accompanied to Walvis Bay by a German Namibian ornithologist, Bernhard Rossenthal. What Mothinsi had told Charles about the abundance of birdlife on the huge lagoon turned out to be accurate. Rossenthal was able to identify many bird species that Charles was unable to recognise, which he was quick to record on his checklist. And whilst kayaking out to Pelican Point, when they had been guided through three colonies of fur seals, with flocks of gulls and cormorants overhead, Rossenthal pointed out the two different types of dolphins that they had encountered, the Heaviside's and the Bottlenose dolphin.

Charles had spent his last days Swakopmund carefully checking through all the data that he had been able to glean about the Herero tribe from the Sam Cohen archives. In appreciation of all the help that Kakuii had given him during his time at the museum, he took him, his wife and two daughters for a farewell dinner at one of the town's favourite eating places, the Tiger Reef Beach Bar & Grill. The views of the turbulent waves of the ocean, and the sand dunes of the Namib Desert, were difficult to surpass. As he watched the spectacular sun sinking behind the sea, Charles thought that it could not have been more of a contrast to the view from the orangery at his family home of Hartlington Hall, over the Home Park, the lake and beyond to the undulating moorlands of the Yorkshire Dales.

9

SKEINS OF CORRUPTION

Just two days before Charles was to catch the Swakopmund train to Windhoek, he received a message, via Kakuii, from his police superintendent friend in Okahandja. The superintendent had requested him to stop off there for a few days, as he had some important information about Megano Angelo which he would like to share with him. He also required more background information about Megano's involvement with the mineral deposit find near Nxau Nxau, and his association with Jefta Kandorozu. This was a request that Charles was only too happy to agree to.

At Okahandja, Charles took a taxi from the station and returned to the Sylvanette Guest House, where he managed to have the same room that he had shared with Christiane; how very much he wished that she were with him there. It was the same evening of his arrival that he had his first meeting with Police Superintendent Heinz Klös, who had joined him at a secluded corner of the patio where they were able to share a beer and a snack together. Charles was impressed by the way this tall, self-assured and handsome middle-aged Namibian of

German descent introduced himself and did not immediately launch into the main reason for their meeting. Instead, Heinz had asked him about the times that he had spent with his friend, Kakuii, in Swakopmund, about his studies of the Herero tribe, and they soon got onto Christian name terms.

'Charles, since my crime investigation department placed a tail on Megano Angelo, we have been able to discover a considerable amount about what have turned out to be his subversive activities in Namibia. And these particularly have been with regards to his direct involvement with a Chinese company, Bazhong Hangheng Plc, which has its headquarters in this country, in Windhoek. Also, during his absence from his lodgings here in Okahandja we took the opportunity to go through his belongings – these have provided us with a considerable amount of incriminating material, which we have copied. I should like to let you see some of this, for you could possibly know some of the persons referred to.'

Whilst Charles ordered another beer for them both, he took the first of the copied letters from the superintendent, and was surprised to note that it was correspondence between his Chinese Gumare friend, Zhang Jinchu, and Angelo, which had been delivered to him via the office of his employees, Bazhong Hangheng in Windhoek. Although the letter had been marked 'Private', 'Registered' and 'To be forwarded', Heinz told Charles that it had been impossible for him to determine whether anyone at the mineral company's headquarters had gained access to its content.

Charles carefully read through the correspondence, while Heinz kept a direct eye on his reaction to what he was reading. After Charles had taken a further sip of his lager he said, 'Yes, I did consider that Zhang Jinchu was a friend of mine during my time in Botswana – I introduced him to Nxau Nxau's tribal chief, Moagi Tjamuaha. And this introduction resulted in Jinchu's mining company here in Namibia being given sole mineral exploration rights throughout the region that falls under Chief Moagi's jurisdiction. However, I see from the correspondence that this fortunately has nothing to do with the agreement between Chief Moagi and Bazhong Hangheng Plc but is rather to do with Zhang Jinchu's offer to Angelo to market, through his connections, any gemstones that he may be able to get his hands on. Also, I noted Jinchu stressed that such transactions would result in them having a significant financial reward for themselves, rather than the profits going to the vendor, and that one of these obvious illicit gemstone deals has already taken place.'

'Charles, no doubt you will be surprised to hear that it is evident from the correspondence Zhang Jinchu has visited Angelo in Windhoek and arranged for him to meet a colleague of his by the name of Alguro Chen, who is also employed by BH Plc, and is operating here in Namibia. Also, after we had carried out extensive checks on Chen's and Jinchu's backgrounds, we found that they had both graduated at the same time from their Mining and Technology degrees at Xuzhou University.'

'How do you plan to deal with this?'

'My department is continuing to keep a close eye on all the movements of both Jinchu and Chen and is currently carrying out investigations on the people they have been associating with,' Heinz replied. 'Also, one factor from our observations is very clear, that we are only touching the edge of a major Chinese network of illicit transactions, and that Alguro Chen is a major player in such corrupt dealings. These have not only involved Chen passing on valuable gemstones to Angelo, and him trafficking these to your friend Jinchu in Botswana but also, from our investigations, Chen has been found to be in the process of negotiating with some subversive tribal elders and local government officials the acquisition of various mineral mining rights in a number of different sites throughout the country.'

Heinz paused, looking directly at Charles. 'What is now of the utmost importance,' he continued, 'is for our police department to be given more time for our enquiries, before arresting Angelo and returning him to Botswana to face trial. In the first instance, it is very much thanks to you having recognised Megano Angelo in the Amaegoesab Bar that we have been able to embark on such a major investigation, the result of which could well turn out to be one of the largest cases of corrupt dealings by foreign corporations involved in the illegal trading and theft of our country's mineral wealth.'

'Heinz, I fully appreciate the importance of your department being given as much time as possible to gather sufficient incriminating evidence,' Charles replied. 'However, I hope you appreciate that when I return to Botswana next month, it will be my duty to report to the Botswana police service that I spotted Angelo in a bar at Okahandja. And, as a consequence, I gave a statement to your police force that the Botswana police had issued a warrant for Angelo's arrest in connection with his previous close association with Jefta Kandorozu, currently in prison facing a charge of murder. If I were not to do so, I could well be arrested myself for having concealed such important information from the Botswana police, which could in turn influence the proceedings of the forthcoming murder trial of Kandorozu.'

The following morning, Charles was picked up by a police car and driven to Heinz Klös's office at police headquarters.

Once Charles was seated, Heinz slid an envelope across the highly polished mahogany desk. 'In the envelope is a transcript which covers the conversation that we had together last evening, as well as a formal request to the Botswana Police Service for us to delay arresting Megano Angelo, and return him to Botswana for the reasons that we discussed last night.'

Charles picked up the envelope and waited for Heinz to continue.

'This morning, I have transmitted the enclosed documentation via South Africa using Interpol's secure internet to my senior police counterpart in Gaberone. I am now waiting for a response from either him, or perhaps from another member of the Botswana Police Service who is more directly connected with Kandorozu's forthcoming murder trial in Gumare. As I am confident that I shall receive a quick response to my communication from my Botswana colleagues, I should like this evening to meet up with you again at the Sylvanette Guest House in order to let you know their response to my request, and this time the drinks and dinner will be on me.'

On his way back to the Sylvanette, Charles called in at the post office to put through a call to Christiane. He was surprised to hear a recorded message to say that she was away from Windhoek for a few days and would not be returning until the following Monday. The message puzzled Charles greatly; Christiane had made no previous mention of planning to be away from Windhoek when Charles had phoned her quite recently from Swakopmund.

That evening, Heinz Klös was as punctual as ever, for he had previously informed Charles that he always made sure he would never take a sundowner prior to 6pm, such was the regimented mind of the superintendent.

'Charles, no doubt you will be delighted to hear that the Botswana Police Service have given us some further time to carry out our investigations, prior to our arrest of Angelo on their behalf, and they have started the legal extradition procedure. However, from our recent observations it appears that Angelo is only a very small cog in Alguro Chen's quite broad network of clandestine transactions. He is only involved with the trading of valuable gemstones with Angelo, he in turn being able to smuggle these to your friend Zhang Jinchu, in Botswana.'

'I don't think that we can call Zhang my "friend" any more, Heinz,' Charles interjected. 'I think he had his own motives for seeking out my acquaintance.'

'I think you may well be right,' Heinz continued. 'As you will have read in the transcript, I recorded how you, after having recognised Kandorozu in a bar in Okahandja, had immediately reported the sighting of a "wanted person" to the police here and so you were responsible for setting the whole of this major investigation in motion. As a part of their response to my request, they have mentioned that as you are acquainted with both Kandorozu and Angelo, you will be required to appear as a prosecution witness at the murder trial, which is due to take place in Gumare in just over a month's time. As you are a British citizen, they have informed the British High Commission in Gaberone of your involvement in this case and have asked us to do the same, in the strictest confidence, with your High Commission in Windhoek.'

After they had finished going over the 'pros and cons' of the response that Heinz received from Botswana, they spent the rest of the evening having what turned out to be a most enjoyable time. They talked about everything but the criminal investigations that were currently underway. Although, on leaving the guesthouse Heinz embraced Charles and said, 'Once all of this major crime investigation is over, and you have returned home to Great Britain, you must make contact with me again so that I can let you know exactly what ultimately transpires. As I have mentioned to you before, it is very much thanks to you for having alerted us to Kandorozu's presence in our country that we had the lead to the wealth of criminal activities taking place here that were previously unnoticed. I have every hope that after the result of further investigations, we shall be able to secure a number of successful criminal prosecutions of both foreign nationals and local people who are currently exploiting Namibia's mineral wealth.'

When Charles returned to his room, his first thoughts were about the absence of Christiane from it and how puzzled he was becoming about her unexpected disappearance from Windhoek. Then his mind became preoccupied with all the ramifications of him in all probability having to be involved as a prosecution witness in the murder trial of Esther Ochuros in Gumare, in the quite near future; the participation of Zhang Jinchu in the illicit marketing of contraband gemstones; and with his confidential connections with both Barrie Hicks and Colin Patterson at the British High Commissions in Windhoek and Gaberone. But that night he could only dream about being in the arms of his dearly loved one, Christiane.

On the following Monday morning, Charles caught the train to Windhoek and returned to the Country Club. Here, he tried once more to make contact with Christiane but was only to hear the same recorded words, so he left a message to let her know that he was now back in Windhoek and staying at the Country Club. As Charles was becoming increasingly concerned, he contemplated phoning the High Commission but, on second thoughts, decided to leave it for another twenty-four hours. In the meantime he would try to make contact with her again by phoning later on in the day in the hope that she had, by then, returned. But, if that didn't happen, he planned to go around to her embassy accommodation in order to see whether there were any messages or clues to her whereabouts.

Following the procedure that Barrie Hicks had established, to only communicate with him directly if he considered it to be of the utmost importance for them to discuss matters face to face, he phoned Hicks' personal ex-directory secure number. As Hicks was out, he left a message on an answerphone to notify him that he was now back staying at the Windhoek Country Club and that it was urgent for them to meet at the earliest opportunity. After which he unpacked his suitcase, and spent some time assembling his thoughts and writing down in the form of an official statement everything that he could recall of his meeting with Jefta Kandorozu and Megano Angelo in Nxau Nxau, his seeing them both in the bar in Gumare, and the more recent sighting of Megano Angelo in Okahandja.

It had been Superintendent Heinz Klös who had recommended him to do this, for he was sure that the lawyers for both Kandorozu's defence and prosecution would require him to present the police service and themselves with a signed and witnessed statement, prior to the forthcoming murder trial in Gumare. The superintendent had also mentioned that from his communications with the Botswana police, it was unlikely that the murder trial would take place within three months, which had provided him with some more time before arresting Megano and returning him to Botswana to face trial with Kandorozu. He understood that the British High Commission in Gaberone were trying to do everything possible to avoid Charles having to remain in Botswana to be present at the trial, so his affidavit would represent an important factor in this process.

On returning to his room after dinner, on the same day that he had left a message for Barrie Hicks, he found an envelope that had been slipped under his door, with a message that he was to be picked up in the Country Club's car park at 10.30 the following morning. The note had stated that the vehicle would be a dark green Land Rover and had recorded its registration number. Very much to his relief there was a message from Christiane, so Charles immediately called her back.

'Charles, I am so upset to hear from the messages that you left you were so concerned about me, but didn't you receive the long letter that I posted at least two weeks ago to your box-number address in Swakopmund? I told you that completely out of the blue His Excellency the German Ambassador to Namibia and his wife had invited me to be one of their guests to spend a long weekend at a private game reserve. An invitation that would have been impossible for me to turn down and, of course, I could not have been more delighted to accept.'

'I didn't get the letter but I'm just relieved to hear you're safe and sound. Of course, you had to go. Was there anything else in the letter that I should know?'

'I also thanked you for your most descriptive letter about the trips you had made to see the colonies of Cape fur seals, dolphins, flamingos, pelicans and all the birdlife on the lagoon. And I was so jealous to hear about your kayak trip to Pelican Point, which must have been great fun – it all sounded quite adventurous.'

Charles and Christiane continued talking about their respective trips; there was so much to catch up on, he only gave her a brief account of his recent three days with the police superintendent in Okahandja. They arranged to have dinner together at the Country Club on the following evening; Christiane would join him for a sundowner there by 6pm when they would have the opportunity to more fully catch up with all the quite dramatic events that had occurred since their last meeting.

The following morning, the dark green Land Rover turned into the car park punctually, and after the African driver had introduced himself, with a broad smile across his friendly face, Charles was driven for just over half an hour to a spacious-looking thatched farmhouse, very much Dutch Cape architecture. As the vehicle pulled into the cobbled courtyard, Barrie Hicks was there to welcome Charles to the British High Commission's country retreat.

After the usual pleasantries, and Charles being handed a steaming mug of coffee, they immediately got down to business, with Hicks having first checked with Charles whether he would mind if he were to record their conversation, which Charles had readily accepted. 'Barrie, as you are already aware, after I recognised Megano Angelo in the bar in Okahandja the police there have been keeping a close eye on his movements and on the people that he has been associating with. I would first like you to see the document that the police superintendent Heinz Klös, who is handling the investigations, has sent to the police service in Botswana.'

Charles handed over the transcript to Barrie that Heinz had given him.

'You will see from this document that apart from it providing a good insight into Angelo's dealings with a Chinese Alguro Chen, who is considered to be a major cog in a series of irregularities and illegal transactions in Namibia, Klös has asked their permission for a delay in arresting Angelo, and returning him to face the murder trial in Gumare. The communication requests confirmation from them that on my return to Botswana, I shall not in any way face a criminal charge for having withheld information which prevented Angelo's arrest and his subsequent extradition to face the forthcoming murder trial in Gumare.'

Hicks spent some time studying the contents of the police transmission and then brought Charles up to date with the most recent communications he had received from his counterpart in Gaberone, Colin Patterson. 'Very much thanks to the information received from the Namibian police force about Angelo's gemstone dealings with Zhang Jinchu, they have now managed to establish that Zhang passed the gemstone to a postal deposit box in Kitwe in Zambia. Although the Zambian police have managed to find out that Zhang's father, Li Yang Jinchu, lives in Kitwe, and is a senior executive of a major Chinese mining corporation operating there, they have been unable to connect him with the PO box where the gemstone was deposited. However, Patterson believes that through his various contacts in the police service, it will not be too long before the reason for Katsuro Khama's murder and the person who was responsible for it are uncovered.'

After his house boy had placed in front of them two glasses of cold Castle lager, he continued, 'The Batauana police superintendent in charge of the investigation is currently working closely with his Zambian counterpart in the hope of finding out the identity of the person who the gemstone was delivered to in Kitwe. But one thing that they have managed to establish is that at much the same time that Zhang had managed to send the gemstone to Zambia, the Visha Gemstone Trading Corporation in Kitwe had traded an uncut gemstone for US $750,000. Although, after they had examined the Visha's trading ledgers, the only reference that the police were able to find was the mention of the PO box number where the sale amount had to be placed. So, since then, the Zambian police have been keeping a close eye on the activities of a number of foreign gemstone dealers, especially those of Zhang's father, who are operating in the country's Copperbelt. Although Patterson has been told that recently the police service have been monitoring a Chinese citizen, a Benjamin Huang, who has a flat in Gaberone, who they consider could well have had a hand in Katsuro's murder.

'Charles, I shall now tell you about the amount of incriminating evidence with regards to your friend, Zhang, which has only during the last week or so come to light. When the Botswana police raided his flat in Gumare and examined various documents which included some important data that a police computer expert had managed to gain from Zhang's emails, they recorded sufficient incriminating evidence for the police to arrest him.'

Hicks paused to take a sip of the cold beer. 'Now, to really put the icing on the cake of all of these incidences of intrigue, corruption and murder, the police had a calligraphy expert examine the note that Katsuro had found left in his hatband from which the gemstone had been stolen, along with the note that they found amongst Katsuro's belongings threatening him not to attempt to find out how and where his valuable uncut diamond had been stolen from him. It has now been established that both were in Huang's writing, and from what Katsuro's girlfriend then told the police he had paid another visit to Maun and located the girl that had been paid to give him the drugged whisky. He subsequently managed to find out Huang's full name, and that he was based in Gaberone.

'Due to the warning that Huang had given Katsuro not to try to discover how the gemstone had been stolen from him, the police now consider that Huang could well have been responsible for Katsuro's murder. No doubt the last thing that Huang wanted was for the whole web of his involvement in criminal activities in Botswana to be revealed. So, the police, last Friday, issued a warrant for Huang's arrest, not only for his illicit trading of valuable gemstones, but also for the murder of Katsuro Khama. Regrettably, at present the police have been unable to locate Huang, although there are various rumours that after he had been informed by one of his neighbours that his flat had been raided by the police, and that they had carried away his computer and a bag of documents, he had fled to either Namibia or Zambia.'

Over an excellent curry lunch which had all the necessary spices, which had been served on the spacious veranda festooned by the vibrant colours of the ubiquitous bougainvillea climbers, overlooking an immaculately striped, recently mowed lawn, Charles could only reflect on just how many clandestine dealings he had become privy to in less than six months since his arrival in Botswana and Namibia. Also, that in all probability he would be required as one of the prosecution witnesses in the trial of Jefta Kandorozu and perhaps of Megano Angelo, for the murder of Esther Ochuros in Nxau Nxau.

While they had coffee, Hicks said, 'You will be pleased to hear that Colin Patterson has informed me that after his meeting with a senior officer of the Botswana Police Service, you will no longer be required to be present at Esther Ochuros's murder trial. However, this is on the understanding that you first provide them with a signed affidavit which, in order to make it a legal document, has to be counter-signed by a senior member of the High Commission, to record everything you observed, to make reference to the nature of your brief encounter with Ochuros and, of course, you having noticed Angelo in a bar in Okahandja. Your identification of him has so significantly aided the Namibia police to identify the subversive criminal activities that are being carried out by foreign companies operating in this country.'

Just before the Land Rover returned to take him back to the Windhoek Country Club, Hicks said, 'Charles, it has been a delight to meet you, and we at the High Commission and the Namibian police are most grateful to you for all the valuable information you have provided us with. You may not be aware, but whenever the police become involved with a foreign national they immediately notify either the Embassy or the High Commission of the person concerned. And, in your case, Superintendent Heinz Klös has kept our High Commission fully informed about the most productive meetings he has had with you.'

'Don't mention it. I must say I'm relieved I no longer have to appear as a witness at the trial, although of course I would have done anything to help convict those responsible.'

'Of course, the affidavit will be far preferable. I know that you are soon to leave Namibia to fly to Gaberone. However, whilst you are in Gaberone, prior to your return to the UK, Colin Patterson will be making contact with you, he will arrange for the one of his senior colleagues at the High Commission to counter-sign your completed affidavit in your presence.'

After returning to the Country Club, Charles showered in preparation to meeting Christiane again, whom he had not seen since their stay together in Okahandja just over three weeks ago. He was saddened that as Christiane was due to fly to Frankfurt on the coming Saturday, they would not have the opportunity of spending the whole of the evenings and nights together during her last forty-eight hours with him in Namibia. But their evening at the Country Club was as enjoyable as ever, with them both bursting with enthusiasm with everything that they wanted to share with each other.

Christiane had arrived by taxi, for since her return from Okahandja she had no longer required the use of the BMW that the German Embassy had loaned to her. The vehicle had been given to a newly arrived member of the embassy staff. So, Charles had ordered a cab to return her to her residence but, at the same time, had told her that he would accompany her to ensure that she ended the evening safely. Also, having fully recognised that the embassy rules disallowed the occupants from entertaining guests in their loaned accommodation, so he would have to return to the Country Club in the same cab.

Charles had chosen a table in a quiet corner of a crowded bar, ordering a half-bottle of Prosecco. For he had always referred to the importance of having what he termed as a good 'smiler' prior to discussing anything at all serious. Christiane had been anxious to tell Charles as much as possible about the long weekend which she had just spent as a guest of the German Ambassador and his wife, with three other members of the embassy staff at the Goche Ganas Private Nature Reserve, just to the south of Windhoek.

'As I mentioned the invitation came totally out of the blue, for I had only previously met the ambassador on one occasion, and although I was quite apprehensive about joining their party, the four days did turn out to be a most enjoyable time. The ambassador, Johan Lutz-Gôtz, and his wife Eve-Maria turned out to be most hospitable and friendly, and evidently they were keen for me to meet a distant relative of mine, a Count Wolfgang von Semmler, who is a descendant from the Semmler-Delmenhorst line of my ancestry.'

'Does the Count live in Namibia?'

'No – in fact Wolfgang had only just arrived on secondment from the Federal German Government for three months, as the

Embassy's Deputy Head of Mission, covering for a fellow diplomat away in Germany on sick leave. The other couple who made up the party were Eva-Maria's younger sister and her husband. The nature reserve, close to Wellness village, was a delightful, wild environment to be in; the chalets were really luxurious, on a hilltop with glorious views. We did several game drives around the nature reserve – we saw white rhino, giraffe, zebra and eland, as well as numerous species of birdlife, including a gathering of ostriches which were almost tame. They would come right up to you, and eat out of your hand if you wanted.'

'Seeing as Wolfgang is a distant relative, did you mention to him why you are here? Your family research?'

'I only made mention to Wolfgang of our prince ancestor on one occasion. I said how delighted I had been to establish that during his time in South West Africa, he had been a great supporter of Theodor Leutwein's liberal approach to his dealings with the indigenous people. Also, how pleased I was to read that on their return to Germany, just after the genocide that General Lothar von Trotha unleashed, they had exerted their influence on both Kaiser Wilhelm II and the German government to put an end to the slaughter, and to have eventually had General von Trotha withdrawn from the colony.'

'Do you think he shared your views?'

'Well, I mentioned it after dinner on the second night of our stay, when all the party seemed to me to be in a very relaxed mood. But when I mentioned "genocide" the ambassador quickly become more alert and said, although he acknowledged the historical realities that a great number of indigenous people were killed in the tribal uprising against the German colonial power, he did not accept that genocide had taken place.'

Christiane explained that the ambassador had continued by saying that the Federal German Government could be proud of having had a special responsibility for Namibia since its independence, particularly by helping its economic viability and governance. But he did make mention of the fact that members of the von Trotha family had quite recently visited Namibia, after having accepted an invitation from the Herero chiefs, and had on behalf of their family apologised for the atrocities that their ancestor had inflicted on their tribe. Also, that he was optimistic his government would continue to make every effort to resolve the situation with regards to being able to find a satisfactory solution to this massacre issue. As well as to whether or not the German government will make an official apology with regards to this slaughter of Namibia's indigenous people. After this exchange, no further references to the German colonial days in this country were made.'

Charles had responded as enthusiastically as possible to what Christiane had just told him. 'What a great coincidence that one of the ambassador's guests turned out to be a distant second cousin of yours. And no doubt he found your investigations concerning one of your mutual relatives to be quite fascinating.'

'Wolfgang has kindly promised that should he during his time at the embassy come across any confidential references to our ancestor's involvement with Theodor Leutwein, or to the events leading up to the massacres that make reference to him, which he considered I would have been unlikely to gain access to, he would be only too happy to send such additional information to me at Schloss Braunschweig.'

Before going into dinner, Charles had ordered another half-bottle of Prosecco and told Christiane just about everything he had been told by Superintendent Heinz Klös since she had left Okahandja. Particularly about how Megano played a very small part in the illegal activities that the Chinese mineral operator, Alguro Chen, had masterminded in the country. Some of his activities had involved not only the trading of valuable uncut gemstones, but also with the establishment of unofficial contracts undertaken with the aid of subversive local government officials and a number of tribal elders in connection with the issue of licences for the Chinese company's exploration of the country's valuable uranium and iron ore deposits. During the rest of the evening, over dinner, they talked about all the most memorable and fun times that they had spent in each other's company during their safari trip to Etosha Pan, the Skeleton Coast, Swakopmund and latterly in Okahandja. They both felt the findings of their respective academic investigations on the Herero tribe and of Christiane's ancestor had been of mutual benefit to their studies. The evening ended with Charles taking Christiane back to her embassy residence by taxi and, after having found it difficult to release her from a long, warm embrace, and kissing her on the lips, he had to most reluctantly return alone to his bedroom at the Country Club.

As the following day was to be Christiane's last, prior to her flight to Frankfurt on the Saturday morning, Charles had arranged to collect her and take her for dinner at the acclaimed five-star JoJo's restaurant in Garten Street. Christiane had told him that the ambassador had insisted the embassy would be responsible for taking her to the airport to ensure that she cleared immigration without any problems; he knew that this would be his last opportunity of being with her in Windhoek.

On hearing this, Charles only hoped that Wolfgang von Semmler would not suggest to the ambassador that he would be pleased to have the opportunity to convey his second cousin to the airport, and to guide her through the immigration formalities. For there was nothing more that he would have wished to do than to be with her at the airport, to embrace and kiss her goodbye, before their next meeting at Durham University.

10

EMOTIONAL ENTANGLEMENTS

Christiane had been due to join Charles at a New Year's Eve party at Barden Towers, the seat of the Earl and Countess of Drysdale, who were close friends of his parents, Dr Mathew and Jan Duncan. However, the day after Boxing Day Charles received a registered letter from Germany, from Christiane. And the letter read:

> *Charles, it almost breaks my heart in having to write this letter to you, but since my return home to Schloss Braunschweig so much emotional disarray and upset has happened to me. But first it is important for me to let you know that I am unable to join you and your parents at the New Year's Eve party with your family friends. Do please try to understand my predicament, for I have loved our many times together since our first meeting in Durham, getting to know each of our families, and more recently the unforgettable safari and other special times in Namibia.*

These will always represent the fondest of memories for me.

However, you may recall that during the long weekend that I was a guest of the German ambassador and his wife at the nature reserve, I met for the first time a distant cousin of mine, Count Wolfgang von Semmler, who had been seconded to the German Embassy for a period of three months. Well, after Wolfgang's return to his duties in Bonn with the Federal Government he made contact with me, in order to say that he had managed to locate some more interesting facts about our mutual ancestor's time in German South West Africa. And he suggested that he would very much like to see me again and to meet my parents, which resulted in them inviting him to come to stay for a weekend at Schloss Braunschweig.

Charles, I feel awful in having to say this to you but since Wolfgang spent that first weekend with us I recognised that there was something very special about him, and since my return home I have been in his company on several occasions and he has recently asked to marry me. However, I have still to accept his proposal for I wanted you to be the first to know about my intention to accept, for I am aware of the depth of your feelings and love for me, which only recently I undoubtedly felt in return. But now, for the second time in my life, after having first falling in love with you, I am now in love with Wolfgang. My parents are extremely fond of him and are very much in favour of him becoming their son-in-law. Whether this is mainly due to Wolfgang having a distant family connection with the aristocratic lineage or, as they told me when I was a girl, that they always hoped if I was ever to get married, it would be to a German citizen, for this has always been the rather nationalistic custom of our family.

> *Charles, please believe me when I say that I have had to muster a great deal of courage to write this letter to you, and I shall only announce my intention to accept Wolfgang's proposal of marriage when I have confirmation from you that you have received this letter. For I have loved you very much, but my emotions have now been overcome and surmounted by my intense feelings for Wolfgang.*
>
> *Please take the greatest care of yourself, and I could not be more grateful to you for all of the most memorable times that we have spent together.*
>
> *With the fondest of love,*
> *Christiane xx.*
>
> *P.S. The blotches on this page are the result of two tear drops, which I hope will at least demonstrate to you just how sad it has been for me to write this letter.*

Being very British and maintaining a tradition of keeping a 'stiff upper lip', Charles was almost the last person to outwardly show his emotions, but having read Christiane's letter within the privacy of his bedroom he could not prevent his eyes moistening with tears. After reading through the letter for the second time he felt absolutely devastated, as if his whole world was crashing down around him, having lost the person whom he loved so much and hoped to marry. He lay down on his bed and sobbed for the first time in his life.

After falling asleep for a while, and then awakening to gather his thoughts and face up to the realities of what had happened to him with the loss of his loved one, he showered, and went down the baronial staircase of Hartlington Hall to join his mother, Jan, for tea in the orangery, clutching Christiane's letter in his hand. Before sitting he handed the letter to his mother saying, 'I have just received this bombshell from dear Christiane, and all I can say is that I am absolutely devastated.' His mother took the letter and read it slowly, whilst Charles rather nervously sipped his cup of tea and picked up a cucumber sandwich.

After having read the letter, his mother got up from her chair, went over to Charles and kissed him on both cheeks.

'Charles, darling, what an awful shock this must be and I feel so sad for you; both your father and I are so well aware how very fond you have been of her, and we too liked her immensely. Regrettably, the unfortunate break-up of relationships – sometimes most unexpected – is often part and parcel of one's early years. When in the future you fall in love again and marry another girl, you will look back on your deep affection for Christiane as an important part of your life and think fondly of the times that you had with her. Although I know it's hard to imagine now, this feeling will pass.'

Jan looked at her dejected son as he sat with his shoulders hunched, looking down. She would have done anything to chase away the pain that had consumed him.

'Charles, I know that you will recall what I told you before you went to university, that my first marriage turned out to be a disaster. As a twenty-year-old, I was far too young to get married to a man twelve years older than myself, whom I thought that I was very much in love with. And, perhaps, I was subjected to a degree of influence from my parents, for before my husband became a casualty of the Bush War he was a celebrated senior officer in the Selous Scouts. During the latter part of my marriage, before my husband was killed, I had the good fortune to have met your dear father. And indeed, if my husband had not lost his life in the conflict I was, without his knowledge, in the process of divorcing him in order to be free to marry your father and, of course, the rest is history.'

After his mother had poured him another cup of tea, Scobie, their golden Labrador, barged his way into the orangery, wagging his tail and nudging the knee of his young master in the hope of benefiting from some titbits from the tea trolley.

'Darling, the only advice that I can give you at this stage of your great sadness is to sleep on the consequences of Christiane's letter, and tomorrow when you can see the light of day through the haze of your emotions to reply, and to be as philosophical as possible. Most importantly you must mention how you had appreciated that she wanted you to know about her engagement to Wolfgang before anyone else. It is important for you to wish her every possible future happiness, obviously with your love.'

Charles looked up at his mother and nodded his agreement. He knew she was right, but he wasn't ready just yet to wish Christiane's happiness with another man.

Soon after New Year, Charles received a rather tearful phone call from Christiane to tell him how grateful she had been to receive his most considerate and understanding communication. She had ended her call, 'Charles, until meeting Wolfgang you were the most important person in my life, and you will always be part of a very significant chapter of my youth that I shall look back on with great fondness. I do very much hope that we can remain good friends, and that our paths will cross again in the not too distant future – perhaps we shall meet when we graduate from Durham.'

Since his return from Southern Africa in late October, Charles had spent the majority of his time in the compilation of a draft of his doctorate thesis, and in late January he returned to Durham University to spend some time going over the data that he had gathered about the Herero tribe with his tutor, Professor Sam Prior. Charles had been told by his father that Philip Eisenberg had been in contact and had said how much he was looking forward to meeting Charles again when he was next at the university.

St Hild and St Bede provided Charles with pleasant two-room accommodation at the college, and Professor Sam Prior had been impressed by the quantity of information that he had recorded in his notebooks and the depth of his research, as well as the significance of his overall findings. As far as Charles was aware, the Professor had not been told anything about his involvements with passing on significant information to the British High Commissions in the countries where he had been studying. During Charles's three weeks back at Durham, Sam Prior had provided him with some excellent advice and valuable guidelines with regards to how his PhD thesis should be presented to his board of examiners, due to take place later on in the year.

So, apart from spending a great deal of time making corrections and fine-tuning the documentation that the PhD board of examiners required, and going back to Sam Prior for further guidance, he was to spend a considerable amount of his time with Philip Eisenberg. Eisenberg had been not only fascinated to hear first-hand about all the events that had taken place during his time in Southern Africa, but had also been able to bring Charles up to date with the majority of the developments that had taken place since his departure from Botswana.

Their first meeting after Charles's return was back in the wood-panelled environs of Chapters' tea rooms. Eisenberg shook Charles warmly by the hand as he arrived at the quiet corner table.

'Charles, I could not be more delighted to see you again, and to say how I very much appreciated the way you communicated so well with our British High Commissions during your travels. My colleagues in MI6 are most appreciative of the additional information they have managed to find out as a result of your observations. And, of course, the police in Botswana and Namibia were also much gratified for your assistance.'

'I was pleased to be of service. It was largely chance that led to me uncovering any information. What I would really like to know is what was the outcome of the murder trial of Esther Ochuros?'

'Regrettably, the Namibia police were unable to locate Megano Angelo, to return him to Botswana to face trial with Jefta Kandorozu, as there were rumours that he had fled to

Angola to subsequently disappear among some of his Herero tribal folk there. However, Kandorozu was given a fifteen-year prison sentence for manslaughter, for the police were unable to provide the lawyers for the prosecution with sufficient evidence to persuade the jury that he had carried out the murder himself. They had come to the decision that Kandorozu, probably along with Angelo, had instructed another, or others, to carry out the gruesome murder on their behalf.'

'At least justice has been done to some degree, although it's a shame Angelo slipped through the net. Hopefully he will surface at some point.'

During the many meetings that Charles had with Eisenberg in his few weeks back in Durham, either over a luncheon or a tea, he was brought up to date with some of the other developments that had taken place since his return home.

It seemed that Heinz Klös's net was closing in on Alguro Chen, with the hope that some other worthwhile prosecutions would be made at the same time. Mothinsi had told Colin Patterson that Bazhong Hangheng Plc, the company employing Zhang Jinchu, had been fined US $100,000 for having one of their employees operating in Botswana on their behalf accused of fraudulent dealings with valuable gemstones, and the government's Ministry of Minerals, Energy and Water Resources had suspended the company's licence to operate in the country for a period of five years. Fortunately, this resulted in Chief Tjamuaha engaging the services of lawyers in Gumare to cancel his contract.

With regards to the murder of Katsuro Khama, the Botswana Police Service established that Benjamin Huang was connected with the stealing of the gemstone from Khama. Once Huang had come under suspicion, the police found that he had an apartment in Gaberone, which they raided. They found some incriminating evidence, linking him with Katsuro in Maun, as well as with a PO box number in Kitwe.

Eisenberg explained that regrettably, Huang had obviously been told about his apartment having been raided by the police, and a warrant for his arrest being issued. This had resulted in him being quick to flee the country, and it was found that he had returned via Hong Kong to China and disappeared without a trace. Unfortunately, the Botswana Police Service found their Chinese counterparts to be totally uncooperative in assisting them in any way to find Huang.

Eisenberg had explained that Khama's girlfriend had told the police he had been certain his precious gemstone had been taken during his final night at the Cresta Riley's Hotel in Maun. The police had interviewed a number of the hotel's staff, finding that Huang had stayed at the hotel at the same time as Khama.

One of the hotel receptionists had told the police about Tonata, who had been seen speaking to Katsuro, as well as to Huang. They had located Tonata and after having given her an agreeable handful of pulas, she told them everything about how she had been asked by Huang to take a drugged whisky to Khama, in order for him to take back what he had told her was a gemstone that had been stolen from him.

Amongst the documents found in Huang's apartment, the police found a note with regards to a visit he had made to Kitwe, and to the town's major mineral trading company, Visha Corporate Services, where they had found in the company's trading ledgers a reference to a now defunct PO box number, which was registered to a Chinese trading company. However, the police had the opportunity to speak to the man who had taken delivery of the gemstone, and when shown a photograph of Huang, he was able to identify him as the person concerned.

The police were told how Huang had given him the PO box number and stated that the money for the sale had to be deposited in US dollars. However, although the police had been unable to definitely identify the source of one of Visha Corporate's major gemstone sales, they were able to establish that it had taken place at much the same time that Megano was known to have sent a valuable gemstone to Zhang Jinchu who, in turn, had managed to have it delivered to Kitwe.

During Eisenberg's last conversation with Charles, he said, 'The only matter now outstanding is for the police to identify the operator in Kitwe, who both Zhang Jinchu and undoubtedly Huang were associated with. However, it is obvious that the police are dealing with a sophisticated and highly devious professional criminal who has covered his tracks extremely well, and perhaps will never be found to face justice.'

Before Charles's return to Hartlington Hall, he visited the Klute nightclub with some of his college friends. He recalled with great nostalgia his first meeting with Christiane, hearing her rather guttural laugh and having been bewitched by her deep blue eyes. How much he wished that she had been here with him, and for them to be dancing with one another. Instead, through his consumption of rather too much real ale, he had become increasingly sad and soporific.

However, the evening was saved when he bumped into one of Christiane's friends with her boyfriend, who had both been on the same Modern Languages BA course as her. Although they had lost contact with Christiane since she had left to carry out her studies in Namibia, they were fully aware of the depth of Christiane's feelings towards Charles. So, the rest of the evening was spent reminiscing about the fun times that they had all spent together. As it would have been rather awkward to explain what had happened, Charles decided not to tell them about Christiane's engagement to Count Wolfgang von Semmler.

Six weeks after Charles returned to Hartlington Hall to continue with the writing-up of his doctorate thesis, his father received a phone call from a Colonel of the Household Cavalry to inform him that his brother, Major Sir Sebastian Duncan MC, had been killed by a roadside blast in Afghanistan's Helmand Province. All the family and household staff had been devastated to receive the news about his tragic death. For Charles's uncle had been much loved by all of his family, as well as having been greatly respected by his fellow officers and men within the Life Guards of the Blues and Royals Household Cavalry in which he had served.

Sebastian was also well liked and popular with his many civilian friends, as well as by Hartlington Hall's estate workers, some of whom had known him throughout his formative years. Soon after the announcement of his tragic death on active service, the flag bearing the Duncan family's coat of arms was hoisted on the top of Hartlington Hall's west wing. And hung forlornly at half-mast. Scobie also sensed that something awful had occurred for he was failing to receive from the majority of the household the usual amount of welcome that he had previously been accustomed to, and ceased to be constantly wagging his tail. One of the ramifications of Sebastian's death was that as he had no children, Dr Mathew Duncan was gazetted in both *The Times* and in *The Daily Telegraph* as the heir to the Duncan baronetcy.

It had taken a further fortnight before the coffins of both the major and the corporal who had been with him when his jeep had been hit by a roadside device, had arrived in the early afternoon back in the UK at the RAF Brize Norton base in Oxfordshire. As the hearses with the two coffins draped with the Union flag were driven slowly through the streets of nearby Carterton, a crowd of about 200 mourners and servicemen braved the rain and wind to line the streets. A party of British Legion standard bearers were present to pay tribute to their fellow servicemen.

When Sebastian's coffin arrived back in Yorkshire it was taken to St Wilfrids Church in the nearby village of Burnsall, where the Duncan family had their place of burial, and an impressive family gravestone. Although Charles's parents knew that Sebastian's regiment were to hold a full regimental memorial service for him at the Household Cavalry Regimental Chapel in a few months' time, they had been most appreciative of the 400 or so people who had attended the burial service in Burnsall.

During dinner on the evening of the funeral, Charles's father had said to his mother, 'Darling, no doubt the memorial service that the Household Brigade are to organise for Sebastian will be on similar lines to the one that was held for Paddy. Charles, perhaps we have not previously told you much about my meeting your dear mother before her husband, Major Paddy Bushney, was killed.'

Turning to Charles, his father continued, 'Both your mother and I have decided that it would be a good thing for me to tell you something about the times of our first meetings in Southern Rhodesia, as well as some of the events that took place during those few years. As you already know, after I had been successful with my PhD dissertation, I decided to continue with the studying of primate species in Southern Rhodesia. And it was in Rhodesia that I met your dear mother, prior to me being caught up and involved with members of Robert Mugabe's freedom fighters during the country's fight for independence from Ian Smith's government of UDI, the Unilateral Declaration of Independence. And of course, it was during this period that I met your Durham University friend, Philip Eisenberg.

'However, while studying a species of guenon monkey on the country's border with Mozambique, I was kidnapped by ZANLA terrorists and taken over the border where I was quite badly treated, especially by having been regularly caned on the souls of my feet, hence the slight limp that this has left me with. ZANLA had kidnapped me in order to try and get me to sign a document to incriminate a locally popular tribal chief, who had yet to speak out in support of Mugabe's ZANLA/PF's political party. They held me in order to get me to record that the chief was passing on information about their cross-border activities to the local security forces. However, this I obviously refused to do, but was thankfully rescued by a three-man team of Rhodesia's highly trained SAS regiment. If their mission had failed, I would undoubtedly have been murdered by my ZANLA captors.'

After they had topped up each of their wine glasses from a fine cut-glass decanter, his father had gone on to say, 'Charles, the saddest part of my rescue was the bittersweet ending to the whole operation from terrorist hands. For your mother's husband, Major Paddy Bushney, whom Jan had once introduced me to, had been a part of the overall rescue operation. The main objective of the small group of Selous Scouts, which had been under his command, was to cause a diversionary action to draw any serious military attention away from the SAS rescue party. So, resulting from the distraction that the Selous Scouts managed to successfully achieve in the blowing up of a bridge over the Zambezi, close to where the river flows into Mozambique, the SAS assault team was able to fly to a small bush landing strip without any major opposition, within striking distance of the hut where I was being held.'

After taking a further sip of wine, he continued, 'And this is when the whole irony of all of the events that surrounded my rescue took place. After Bushney and his team blew up the bridge, he was shot and killed whilst swimming to rescue one of his badly injured soldiers, who had been blown into the water and was drowning. A counter-attack was immediately mounted by the rest of his team, but although they managed to save the wounded corporal, they were only able to retrieve the dead body of their leader. By coincidence, this event had taken place at much the same time that the DHC-2 Beaver carrying my injured self had landed safely at the RRAF base in Umtali.

'Soon after the news of Bushney's death had been released to the press, Ian Smith announced that he was to be the second person to be posthumously awarded Rhodesia's Grand Cross of Valour, the country's highest military decoration for conspicuous bravery by a member of the security forces. So, you can well imagine that the service at Salisbury Cathedral on such a military hero was very well attended, not only by the prime minister and senior politicians but also by many of the senior officers of the security forces and fellow officers and NCOs, both European and African, from the Selous Scouts.

'Regrettably, due to the injuries that had been inflicted upon me during my days in terrorist hands, I was still undergoing hospital treatment so was unable to attend Bushney's funeral service.' He turned towards Jan. 'I recall you later telling me that the Prime Minister, Ian Smith, had attended the funeral, and that you had been seated between your parents in the same row as the Head of the Armed Forces, Lt General Peter Walls, and the government's Minister of Defence, PK van der Byl. Also, how Lieutenant-Colonel Reid-Daly, the officer commander of the Selous Scouts, had given a moving eulogy about the significant and courageous career of his former colleague, covering not only his brave achievements in the Bush War, but also when he had served with the Rhodesia African Rifles in counter-terrorist activities during the regiment's time with the British Army in the Malayan Emergency.'

'I have already told Charles about having started divorce proceedings, without his knowledge, before him being killed on active service,' Jan said. 'But yes, in spite of this, I did find his funeral service to be a most moving event. I was particularly emotionally overcome whilst listening to Reid-Daly's eulogy, which so well highlighted all of his military achievements and all the gratifying sentiments, and condolences, that had been expressed by so many. How I wish I had been able to prevent myself from sobbing, but it was really an overwhelming occasion.'

Jan had left the dining table and taken a decanter of port from the sideboard, placing it carefully down in front of her husband, and after kissing them both, she excused herself to retire for the night. No doubt to allow the father and son to enjoy the vintage port, and to be free to reminisce about their various experiences of life, and perhaps even on other matters that they may well had on their minds.

*

In late July, Charles returned to Durham University to present his doctorate thesis to the board of examiners, which among its members included Professor Sam Prior, but was chaired by a Professor of Anthropology from the University of Stirling in Scotland. Soon after the examination by the academic body of three professors and two senior lecturers had taken place, his tutor told him that he had done an excellent job in disseminating the data that had made up his written thesis. The board had been most impressed by the high standard of his presentation. So, Sam Prior had told him, in confidence, that he had every hope that it would not be too long before he would hear from the university that he had successfully gained his PhD which, of course, he could not have been more pleased to hear.

The impressive memorial service for his uncle had taken place at the Household Cavalry Regimental Chapel in Knightsbridge, at 11.30 on a cold October morning, which had been accompanied by all the pomp and ceremony always performed for the formal farewell of an officer of the Blues and Royals. Particularly, for an officer of such high repute as Major Sir Sebastian Duncan, MC. At the reception that had followed the service at the Cavalry and Guards Club in Mayfair, Charles had the opportunity to be in the company of many members of his family, some of whom he had not previously had the opportunity to meet.

Soon after Charles's return to Hartlington Hall, he was to receive Durham University's official notification that he had been awarded his Doctor of Philosophy degree. So, Charles was now able to record a PhD with his previously awarded academic achievements of a BSc and MSc.

The news of her son's academic success had prompted Lady Jan Duncan to jokingly tell him, 'I shall now be able to proudly inform all my friends that I have two doctors living with me at Hartlington Hall, although I shall obviously take the precaution of telling them it would be prudent for them to not ask either of you anything about personal health conditions that they may be currently experiencing!'

Charles received his doctorate from the Vice-Chancellor of the University of Durham at a congregation of the university, which assembled in the ecclesiastical surroundings of the early twelfth-century Durham Cathedral, home of the ninth-century Shrine of St Cuthbert. Soon after he had been admitted to his degree, much to his surprise, he received an invitation to present a paper about his studies on the Herero tribe in Botswana and Namibia at the following year's Congress of the International Union of Anthropological and Ethnological Sciences (UAES), which was to take place in Rio de Janeiro, Brazil. Much to his delight, he was to be given a stipend in order for him to participate.

11

A ROBUST REBOUND

Charles was to accompany his father to the AGM of the Yorkshire Dales National Park, which was held at the Park Authority's headquarters at Helmsley, in North Yorkshire. Mathew Duncan had recently been elected to serve on the Park's governing authority, as their family estate represented an important part of the overall Dales National Park. The Duke of Devonshire's nearby Bolton Abbey Estate, and the five-arched bridge at Burnsall, all came under the conservation governance of this important authority that he was now serving on.

As the AGM went on to the late afternoon, they stayed the night at Helmsley's 'olde worlde' Feversham Arms Hotel. After dinner, while they were enjoying a nightcap together, his father said, 'Charles, your mother and I have been most upset for you with regards to Christiane making her decision; we understand it must be very hard on you. However, it may be of help if I were to tell you something about the break-up of my first serious relationship – I was going through the same emotional turmoil that you are in now. Most fortunately, it was only a few months later that I was lucky enough to be introduced to your dear mother, and it did not take too long to put behind me the deep feelings that I had for my first real love in life. So hopefully, this may well become the case for you, although it must be hard to envisage now.'

Charles knew about his mother's first marriage, but his father had never spoken in any depth about his own romantic life, so he sat back in anticipation and waited for him to continue.

'I did, of course, tell your mother all about this previous relationship, for the last thing that I wished to do was to hide any secrets about my previous life from her.' He took another sip of his cognac, casting his mind back thirty years. 'While I was in Zaire, now the Democratic Republic of the Congo, I met a very beautiful and intelligent girl called Lucienne. Her mother was a Belgian citizen; her father had been a medical student from Lubumbashi, Zaire, studying for his medical degree at the same hospital where her mother worked in Brussels. I met their daughter soon after arriving in Bukavu, on the shores of Lake Kivu, where she was working for the Conservator of the Kahuzi-Biega National Park. The place in which you know I spent the majority of my time studying the social interactions of the endangered eastern lowland gorillas.

'During my time in Zaire, we became extremely fond of each other, and I subsequently helped her gain a grant from the renowned primatologist Professor Dr WC Osman Hill, to undertake a degree course at Emory University where, as you know, I did my doctorate degree course. So, when we were in Atlanta, we spent a great deal of our time together. It was only during the latter part of this that we both came to the conclusion that due to our very different backgrounds, preferred lifestyles and ambitions, on my return to the UK it would be best for both of our sakes for our romantic relationship to come to an end. No doubt similar to how you are feeling, our decision to part did cause both of us a great deal of emotional upset which initially, I found most difficult to cope with.

'Several months after we separated in Atlanta, I received a letter from her, posted from an address in Washington, DC, telling me that she recently had married an African-American diplomat, whom she had first met at a reception at the Zaire Embassy in Washington. Also, that she was now pregnant with their first child.

'She told me that her husband was currently posted to the African Section of the State Department in Washington. She mentioned in the letter being amused when her husband told her that all the staff working at this governmental headquarters referred to the department fondly as "Foggy Bottom". However, in moving to Washington she had to give up her degree course at Emory, although she stayed in Atlanta long enough to complete her literary research contract with Dr Osman Hill.

'After Atlanta, I only met this girl on one occasion, and that was after her husband had been posted to the American Embassy in Lusaka. She sent me a note in Salisbury from Lusaka, telling me that she was planning a trip to Victoria Falls with her two children, a son and a daughter, and was there any chance I could fly up to Livingstone to meet the three of them there which, for old time's sake, I agreed to do. So, as she was only visiting her husband in Lusaka for a short stay, he arranged for an embassy chauffeur-driven car to bring her down to Livingstone ostensibly, as far as he was aware, for his two children to see one of the world's greatest wonders, the magnificence of Victoria Falls. The children were a delight to meet, and they both marvelled at the great sheets of water cascading down to the cataracts below. Charles, I do hope that one day you too will have the opportunity to see it, it is a magnificent spectacle.'

The night porter topped up their brandy glasses and his father continued with the reminiscences of his early days in Africa. 'During my lunch with them in Livingstone, I told Lucienne all about how I had fallen in love with your dear mother, and how I hoped that if she was successful in gaining a divorce from her over-jealous and controlling husband, I very much hoped to marry her. Our meeting in Livingstone was the last time that we have been in contact with each other – it was most reassuring to see that Lucienne was happily settled with two delightful children. So, although I was extremely upset at the time of the breaking up of our relationship in Atlanta, I could not have been more fortunate to then meet and fall in love with your mother. And it is, of course, both of our wishes that once you have managed to get over your deep feelings for Christiane, you too will be lucky enough to find a girl of your dreams and wish to marry her.'

Charles had remained quiet while his father had been sharing his reminiscences of his life in Africa. Knowing how happily married his parents were, it did give him hope that he could one day get over losing Christiane.

The following morning, on their return home, Charles thanked his father again for talking to him so candidly. 'Father, I do hope that what happened to you when you met someone else will be the same for me, although at the moment, I can't imagine having any interest in anyone else but Christiane.'

Charles was impressed by the amount of documentation that he received from the offices of the International Union of Anthropological and Ethnological Sciences. Particularly to read the statement from their congress of three years previously that 'No discipline is more important for teaching people about themselves and others, and how they live together in the next century, than anthropology' and the importance that the Union attached to the public dissemination of anthropological research prospective. Charles only hoped that his first major conference presentation about his comparative work on the Herero tribes in Botswana and Namibia, to the largest forum of his discipline in the world, with members from more than fifty countries, would be of a high enough standard for him to impress his anthropological peers.

Sir Mathew and Lady Duncan were with Charles during the University of Durham's Congregation when he was admitted by the university's Vice-Chancellor to his Doctor of Philosophy degree, in the impressive ecclesiastic environment of Durham Cathedral. After Charles received his much-valued degree, his parents told him how impressed they were by the way the university had organised the whole event and added, to Charles's considerable satisfaction, how proud they were of the professional way that he presented his paper, and expressed his gratitude to the Vice-Chancellor, and to the university's academic staff for all of their help and guidance.

Soon afterwards, Charles decided to accept an invitation from Professor Sam Prior to join his team of academics, and he was happy to sign a one-year contract to become a Teaching Fellow at Durham University's Department of Zoology. As the Rio congress was due to take place in July, when the students were down from their studies, his university appointment would provide him with sufficient time, after the congress was over, to spend some of his teaching salary on a post-congress tour. The tour's itinerary included a visit to the world's largest tropical wetlands, the Pantanal and to see the renowned spectacle of the Iguaçu Falls, on Brazil's border with Argentina.

Charles very much enjoyed his time back in Durham and found his teaching duties to be quite stimulating, particularly the variety of questions that the students asked, and he soon recognised that he was still very much on a learning curve. Although occasionally, when visiting old haunts like the Klute nightclub, he could still not help himself reflecting on the most romantic times that Christiane and he had enjoyed in Durham some eighteen months ago.

At the same time Charles submitted an abstract of his paper for publication in the prospectus of the forthcoming Anthropological Congress, he enclosed a cheque in order to secure a place on the post-congress tour to Southern Brazil. He found time to write some further papers, for his father always told him that should he decide to continue with his university teaching career, with an ultimate objective of becoming a Don, he should continue with his research activities and have his findings published in as many scientific peer-reviewed journals as possible.

Before Charles flew to Brazil he was delighted to receive a letter from Superintendent Heinz Klös, who had promised to let him know about the outcome of his extensive investigations into Alguro Chin's network of clandestine dealings, which had been found to have involved both subversive government officials and some senior tribal elders. The superintendent wrote:

In total, we managed to arrest fifteen people who were all found to be directly involved with illicit gemstone transactions, as well as some of them having managed to gain unofficial sole mineral exploration rights on tribal lands. Although, as you have already been informed, prior to his arrest Megano Angelo managed to escape to Angola, but we since established that Angelo was only a very small cog in Alguro Chin's overall operation. However, at the trial Alguro Chen was jailed for a period of twenty years, and his criminal associates received sentences ranging from five to fifteen years. And, as both your previous friend Zhang Jinchu in Botswana, and Chen, were employees of Bazhong Hangheng Plc, the government has rescinded their corporation's permit for them to continue to operate in Namibia.

Charles, I shall always be most indebted to you for having given me, and my police colleagues, the initial source of our lengthy and extensive investigations, which has subsequently brought all of those involved to justice.

Charles arrived in Rio three days before the start of the congress, which was to be held at the five-star Belmond Copacabana Palace Hotel, although he was booked into the more reasonably priced Novo Mondo Hotel at Flamengo, midway between the city and the famous brilliant white-sanded Copacabana beach, overlooked by numerous luxurious hotels. Charles's chief reason for arriving at Rio a few days early was not only to become acclimatised to the region's high temperatures and humidity, but that two of Rio's most famous landmarks, the Sugar Loaf and the Corcovado, were not included in the itinerary of the post-congress tour.

He was fortunate to have been given a room on the south side of the hotel, which overlooked a small side road and park with two impressive lines of tall palm trees. When it became dark with tropical suddenness, he was able to see to the north-west the floodlit outstretched arms of the massive statue of Christ the Redeemer, on the summit of the 2,000-foot peak of the Corcovado. And to the south-east, he saw the similarly floodlit rock of the Sugar Loaf, which looked as if it guarded the entrance to the immense natural harbour of Guanabara Bay. Charles had been fascinated to read that when the Portuguese had first entered the bay in January 1502, they had thought they had found the estuary of a major river. And from this mistake the city got its name Rio de Janeiro, the River of January.

During the single-track rail journey up through the Tijuca forest to the Corcovado peak, he was able to see the unorganised conglomeration of the hovels that form the favelas, inhabited by a large number of Rio's population of over seven million. But on reaching the viewing platform at the base of the statue of Christ the Redeemer, he was able to look over one of the most dramatic urban panoramas in the world where, after the side of the mountain falls away sharply, he could see almost the whole of the city in its naturally beautiful setting.

Charles also found the cable car trip to the top of the Sugar Loaf to be a well worthwhile experience. While ascending and seeing the massive rock in front of him, he recalled the dramatic scene in one of James Bond's films when a fight had taken place on top of the roofs of the cars. Once on the rock's summit he looked to the south, to the beaches of Copacabana and beyond to Ipanema. He could see to the west the commanding massive statue of Corcovado, which kept reappearing between the passing clouds.

One night, just after he had fallen asleep, he was woken by the telephone by his bedside and, on picking up the receiver, he thought he heard the words, 'Want a message?' And when he sleepily asked what the message was about, much to his amusement the lady had replied in broken English, 'No, no, no. Not a message, but you want massage?' An invitation that Charles was quick to decline.

To Charles, Rio de Janeiro could not have been more of a contrast to the cities of Durham, Gaberone and Windhoek. After having explored much of the city and taken walks along the black-and-white zig-zagged paved promenade of Avenida Atlântica, he was able to witness just how affluence and poverty appeared to go hand-in-hand. In some places he noticed children begging for scraps of bread by the open-air cafés, and some pathetic wretches lying on park benches with empty beer cans or bottles by their side. He saw women squatting on pavements and begging, beneath the towering buildings of the city's big banks, where no doubt deals worth millions upon millions of dollars took place each day. As Charles found such incidents of extreme poverty and wealth difficult to comprehend, he was pleased for the proceedings of the congress to get underway, and to preoccupy his mind with the traditions and cultures of the Herero tribal dynasty.

A banner hanging on the wall above the congress registration desks at the Belmond Copacabana Palace Hotel read: 'World Anthropologists and Privatization Engaging Anthropology in Public'. According to the documentation in the registration packet, up to 3,000 participants were expected to attend the congress. Well over a hundred symposia had been grouped in twenty-seven thematic fields of ethnology and anthropology, with some of them due to take place at other hotel and conference venues within the vicinity of the Copacabana. Charles was relieved to see that his presentation about the Herero tribes was to take place on the third day of the congress, at the Palace Hotel.

After Charles marked the presentations that he particularly wanted to listen to, he found the majority of the papers of the six-day congress to have been most stimulating, which had helped his decision to continue with his university teaching career. He'd been fascinated to hear how some of the research papers had highlighted the diversity of the methodology that the authors had used to arrive at their scientifically based conclusions. He was delighted by the way his paper had been received, and the amount of meaningful questions that followed its presentation.

At the conference's farewell dinner-dance at the Copacabana Palace Charles first saw what he considered to be one of the most attractive members of the fairer sex that he had ever set eyes upon. This was when a seemingly constantly smiling young black lady had taken to the dance floor to carry out an impromptu dance. Her straight, slender body had moved elegantly, with the bending of one knee at a time, and taking short steps, to the pounding heartbeat and pulse of the drumming of an African samba. Her long, curly dark hair hung loosely over her shoulders, and her slim neck was blessed by a white choker with a sparkling aqua-marine stone at its centre, which contrasted magnificently with her dark-brown skin. As well as with her stunningly vivid yellow short dress, tied at the waist by a colourful tasselled belt which, in turn, accentuated the curves of her shapely body.

When the young lady left the dance floor, she received a round of applause from some of her fellow diners which, of course, included Charles's enthusiastic clapping. How he wished that he had been brave enough to go over to her table and invite her to dance with him, but he was the first to recognise that dancing was not his forte in life. So after the congress dinner had come to a close, with the traditional gathering of people singing the customary 'Olde Lang Syne', Charles was of the opinion that this was to be the last time that he would ever be able set his eyes upon this stunning young lady.

Two days after the end of the congress, Charles was one of the first to arrive at the offices of the tourist company that had arranged the itinerary for the post-conference visit to the Pantanal and Iguaçu Falls. He was told at the time of the congress that as about fifty people had registered to participate on the visits, the tour operator had decided to break up the numbers into two groups, one to visit the Pantanal first, and then to travel down to Iguaçu, and the others to do the trip in reverse. Charles had been greatly surprised when one of the last people to arrive at the tourist office had been the beautiful young lady whereas he had seen dancing the samba, two nights previously. He could not have been more delighted to find that she was placed in the same party as him.

It did not take long for Charles to enter into a conversation with her, as well as managing to arrange to sit next to her on the coach trip to the airport. She introduced herself as Polly Olingo and told Charles how very much she had enjoyed his paper on the Herero tribe, and was keen to ask him many questions about the time he had spent in South West Africa.

Charles rather nervously responded, 'I saw you perform an impressive samba at the Palace Hotel the other evening – it was really quite sensational. Are you a professional dancer?'

'No, although I love dancing, I am in no way a professional – I am currently studying for a degree in Animal Communication and Behaviour at the University of Maryland's Department of Zoology, in the US.'

Polly explained that her family home was at Chevy Chase in the neighbourhood of Washington, DC, but the only reason that she could afford to attend the congress was that her father was currently serving as the Cultural Secretary at the US embassy in Brasilia. As they could see that they had a great deal in common, they arranged to be seated next to each other on the Varig Airline flight down to Curitiba.

During their party's three-day stay at the Pantanal Ranch Mena Luna Hotel, and their visit to the world's largest wetlands, they had shared the first of what soon turned out to be many enthusiastic embraces, for Charles had found himself totally bewitched by Polly's company. Whilst visiting various parts of the wetlands they had been enthralled by the variety of wildlife that they were able to witness, which ranged from sounders of the white-lipped peccary, rhea, the strikingly plumed Hyacinth macaw, to the numerous Pantanal caiman. By the time they arrived at the five-star Belmond Hotel dos Cataratas at Iguaçu, as far as other members of their twenty or so strong group were concerned, the two of them appeared to have become inseparable. They took many photographs of each other in front of the dramatic series of separate waterfalls and cataracts, which together form the largest waterfall system in the world, and took the opportunity to go on a small boat trip close to the cauldron beneath the Devil's Throat canyon where, in spite of being covered by plastic waterproofs, they both became soaked to the skin.

On the last night of their holiday, Charles became overwhelmed by the extreme happiness that he was experiencing in Polly's company, and how much he regretted that they would soon have to separate. Whilst they were enjoying an after-dinner drink on the hotel's veranda, reminiscing about the great times they had just experienced together, Charles was overcome by his emotions. 'Polly, I know that we have only just met, but I have become crazy about you and just wonder whether you would ever consider marrying me?'

The offer took Polly completely by surprise, but they got up and embraced, immersed in their powerful feelings for each other.

Eventually, Polly pulled away and said, 'Charles, I think that I have fallen in love with you too, but at this stage of our relationship we must not allow our emotions to get the better of us. Also, we're on vacation here it's important for us to spend more time together and to get to know each other much better, before taking such a major step in our lives.'

Charles kissed her again, and almost apologised for having made such an unexpected offer of marriage to her. 'Yes, I know what you have just said is right, and I have obviously allowed my love for you to get the better of me – so, let us see how we can plan in the future to spend as much time as possible in each other's company.'

Polly added, 'My darling mother has often told me that vacation romances, no matter how enjoyable they may be at the time, are more often than not doomed to failure. So, let us just see what the future will have in store for us both.'

Whereupon Charles embraced her again. 'I feel sure that our relationship will prove to be an exception to the rule.'

They returned to their seats to continue reminiscing about the various places they had visited, and their ambition to see as much of each other as they could manage in the future. Also to enjoy a further nightcap of Brazil's national cocktail, a caipirinha on the rocks and to listen to the noise of the Iguaçu River in the background as it tumbled over the edge of the Paraná Plateau, on the Argentine side of the falls, to the cataracts and chasms beneath.

On their return flight to Rio the following morning, Polly said, 'Charles, before leaving the hotel I phoned my mother, in order to let her know my flight arrival time in Brasilia this evening. During our conversation I told her something about you, what wonderful company you have been throughout our vacation, and that you had told me how very much you wanted to see me again. So, my mother said, why not ask him to visit us in Brasilia? Apart from us being together again, it is a city well worth seeing. And she and my father would love to meet someone who has made me so happy!'

'What a wonderful idea, but I'm due to return to the UK in two days' time – let me see how much it would cost for me to postpone my ticket for three to four days, so that I can fly up to Brasilia to see you. And, of course, to meet your parents!'

During the flight to Rio, Polly told Charles some more about her family. 'My father, Daniel Olingo, is a career diplomat, currently at the US embassy in Brasilia, as you know. My father's ancestors had been brought from West Africa in the late eighteenth century to the New World from West Africa, to work as slaves on the cotton plantations in America's Deep South.

'My mother's father, Dr Gaston Luzembo, was an African medical doctor from Lubumbashi in Katanga Province, in what is now known as the Democratic Republic of the Congo. He met my grandmother, a Belgian nurse, while she was working at the same hospital in Brussels where he studied for his medical degree. I have an elder half-brother, Marcus, who is currently doing a law degree at Yale University. And when not at college, in the absence of our parents, he too lives with me at our family home at Chevy Chase, which one day I hope you will have the opportunity to visit.' Charles thought there was something familiar about the story of Polly's parents, but he soon forgot about it as it was his turn to talk about his family.

Considering his response, Charles decided that it would be out of order for him to make any reference to the Duncan family's hereditary title. Instead, he chose to say, 'My father, Dr Mathew Duncan, gained his PhD at Emory University in Atlanta, Georgia, after his field studies on the endangered eastern lowland gorillas in what was then Zaire. For the last twenty or so years he has been running our family's eighteen hundred-acre estate in the Dales of Yorkshire, in the north of England. My mother, Jan, is of Afrikaner ancestry, born in South Africa and brought up in Zimbabwe, where she met my father in the late 1970s. They were married soon after my mother's first husband was killed while on active service. I am their only son and have no siblings. I hope you can visit us in Yorkshire; it really is a beautiful part of England, and I know my parents would be thrilled to meet you.'

After they had arrived in Rio, there was time to have lunch together before Polly caught her plane to Brasilia. Charles told Polly that he had reserved a room for two nights at the Hotel Novo Mondo, and said, 'Tomorrow, I shall see whether I am able to delay my return to the UK by three or four days, and I promise that I shall let you know within twenty-four hours. I can't bear the thought of having to part from you so suddenly, like this. I would love to be in your company for a few more days.'

Polly had given him two contact telephone numbers, telling him that he was sure to be able to get through on one or the other.

The following morning Charles was successful in changing his BA return ticket to the UK without too much extra cost. He phoned Polly to tell her the good news and that he would now try to secure a flight to Brasilia. Later in the afternoon he purchased a return Rio-Brasilia-Rio ticket on a late evening Varig flight to the capital, that day. He managed to reserve a room for a three-night stay at the reasonably priced Candango Aero Hotel, and early the following morning he gave Polly a considerable surprise by phoning and telling her that he was already in Brasilia, and how very much he looked forward to seeing her at the earliest opportunity. Charles much enjoyed the evening that he spent with her parents, Daniel and Lucienne Olingo, at their spacious apartment within the precincts of the US embassy and found them both to be most welcoming and hospitable. Her father was particularly interested to hear as much as possible about his studies on the Herero tribe.

When Charles mentioned that the chief of the tribe at Nxau Nxau had made him an honorary member, he said, 'That is indeed quite a significant honour to have been bestowed upon you as a European, considering the appalling treatment they have received at the hands of colonisers in the past.' Charles promised to mail a number of the papers that he had had published on the Herero tribe, including a copy of his Rio Congress presentation.

Polly's mother, Lucienne, showed particular interest in hearing about his upbringing at Hartlington Hall, and the nature of the type of work that his father had to undertake in the running of the family estate. Charles had provided her with as much information as possible about his parents and the environment in which he had been most fortunate to spend his formative years. However he decided not to make any reference to the recent death of his uncle, or that his father, as the consequence of his elder brother's death, had inherited the Duncan family baronetcy.

On Charles's last day with Polly in Brasilia, they decided that on their way to the airport they would pay a second visit to the capital's fine Roman Catholic Cathedral of Brasilia. They held hands and walked through the dark tunnel into the bright space under the building's vast glass-domed roof. The structure reminded Charles of the Roman Catholic Cathedral in Liverpool, many of its architectural features being similar.

Before leaving the cathedral they both knelt together under the sculptures of three angels that were suspended over the nave by steel cables to say a prayer. Their parting at the airport was extremely emotional, with them being loath to separate from their embrace when the last call for Charles's flight to Rio had been made. But they promised to keep in regular contact with each other and to arrange, at the earliest opportunity, to be in each other's company once more.

12

AN EXPLOSIVE CONFESSION

After Charles had returned to the UK from Brazil and had spent a few weeks at Hartlington Hall with his parents, the postman delivered a registered envelope addressed to Dr Mathew Duncan. The letter bore a US postal cancellation stamp, and had been clearly marked 'Private & Confidential'. Soon after Mathew had had lunch with Jan, he took the letter to read within the privacy of his study. And how explosive the letter turned out to be.

***

Mrs Lucienne Olingo
9 The Close, Delafield Street, Chevy Chase, Maryland
2815, USA
26 October 2006

My dear Mathew,

The last thing I imagined that I would ever be doing

would be writing such a letter to you. It is now over thirty years since we last met, at the time I was driven with my two children, Marcus and Polly, from Lusaka to Livingstone to visit the Victoria Falls and for us to take the opportunity to see one another again. This was the time that my husband, Daniel Olingo, had just taken up his first overseas diplomatic appointment at the US embassy in Zambia. Also, you may well recall after the lunch we had together at a hotel close to Victoria Falls, that you accompanied my two children and me to the Falls' eastern cataract. And, when Marcus became scared by the thunderous noise of the massive sheets of white-water cascading over the precipice of the cataract and main fall, how he had run over to take the hand of someone who was almost a stranger.

However, this letter is not to reminisce about the many memorable times that we shared together in Zaire and Atlanta, but the time has now come for me to make this very major confession to you which, perhaps, I should have done well before now. Mathew, please be assured, that this letter is the first time that I have revealed to anyone, including my husband and Marcus, the identity of his father, and of my first child. However, when I became pregnant with your child, you will well recall the considerable degrees of trauma that we both experienced, prior to us mutually agreeing that it was best for both of us if my pregnancy were to be terminated. Before your return to the UK, you wanted to accompany me to the clinic in San Diego, to provide me with as much support as possible. And how I had declined such a thoughtful gesture and told you how I preferred to face up to such a basic reality of life, on my own.

It was just three days prior to the appointment at the clinic that I was overcome by anxiety and became *extremely emotional, with no doubt my maternal instincts getting the better of me, so I phoned the clinic and cancelled the appointment. So, just over seven months after your departure from Atlanta to return to the UK, our son was born on 16 March. And three months later, he was christened Marcus Luzembo, at Atlanta's St Anthony Padua Roman Catholic Church. However, soon after my engagement to Daniel in Washington DC, and prior to our marriage, he decided that it would be appropriate for him to adopt Marcus, so we have lived as a very happy family since that time. And Polly and her elder half-brother have always been the greatest of friends.*

Polly has told me that she and Charles met soon after she had attended the Anthropological and Ethnological Congress in Rio de Janeiro, at which Charles had presented a paper. Whilst they were both together on a post-congress tour to the Pantanal and to Iguaçu Falls, in Southern Brazil, their romance blossomed. Soon after this, Charles followed Polly up to Brasilia to see her, prior to his flight back to the UK. As Daniel is currently attached to the US embassy in Brazil's capital, we had the opportunity to have him spend an evening with us at our apartment, and we found Charles to be a most delightful and intelligent person, and some of his mannerisms certainly reminded me of you. However, Polly has told me, in the strictest confidence, that during their last evening together at Iguaçu that Charles asked her whether she would ever consider marrying him.

Mathew, at this stage of Charles's and Polly's strong attachment to each other, what should we do? Although, I obviously have avoided speaking to her anything about the 'Subject of Relationships'. Do you think that it would it be wise for us to confess, to Marcus first, and afterwards to all other close members of our two families, that dear

Marcus is the result of the romance we had together during our youth? Or, would it be better for us to just wait to see whether Polly and Charles's romance is to flourish into something more permanent?

Mathew, I am still finding it extremely difficult to get to grips with the irony of this incredible situation, particularly the fact that Polly's half-brother is biologically related to her, although that she has no genetic connection with you. So, please let me know your thoughts on all of this as soon as possible.

With my love to you and Jan, whom I recall you telling me all about at our Livingstone meeting. And once you have managed to collect your thoughts on my predicament, please phone me on my private number, which is recorded on the P.S. overleaf.

With my fondest warm wishes.

As ever, Lucienne.

The content of Lucienne's letter hit Mathew like a thunderbolt. He did recall on Charles's return home from Brazil, that he had mentioned how much he had enjoyed his post-conference trip to the Pantanal and to Iguaçu Falls, how he had met a very beautiful girl whom he had become extremely fond of. He had said that he visited Brasilia to say goodbye to her and had met her parents. But Charles certainly hadn't mentioned anything further about the strength of his relationship with the girl, whom he had only just recently met. After reading the letter over once more, he replaced it in its envelope, and placed it in his safe. And with his emotions reaching a state of disarray, he walked briskly to the stable yard, saddled his grey stallion, Winston, and took him for a gallop across the Home Park.

On returning to the Hall, Mathew went to his office to retrieve the letter from the safe and joined his wife in the orangery to take their customary tea together. Just prior to sitting down with Lucienne's letter in his hand, he said, 'Darling, I have just experienced the greatest shock of my life by discovering from this letter, that I am father to a son whom I have previously known absolutely nothing about. Although I recall that prior to our marriage I told you a great deal about my love affair with Lucienne in Zaire and Atlanta. You will have to forgive me for not having confessed to you that Lucienne discovered that she was pregnant just prior to my return home from Atlanta. Before my departure we had both agreed that it would be best for both of our futures if the pregnancy should be terminated. And this is what has just given me the shock of my life.' Mathew handed the letter to Jan and sat down to grasp his cup of tea.

Mathew could hardly keep his eyes off his dear wife as she slowly read through the letter and read it again. After what had seemed to Mathew to have represented an age of stunned silence, Jan suddenly threw her head back in laughter, got up and went over to Mathew to give him a loving, long-lasting warm kiss.

'Darling, I feel sure that you will remember only too well all the stressful times that we had during that tumultuous period when we had first met in Salisbury, and the extremely unhappy state of my married life there. And, how fortunate it was for me, that you arrived like a crusading knight in shining armour, to rescue me from the misery of that relationship. I can quite understand your dilemma and your wish to meet your son – and I would like to meet him too. As to your response to Lucienne's letter, may I suggest that we sleep on it.'

She kissed him again, and said, 'Darling, it was the angels in heaven who were gracious enough to guide us in the major decisions which we had to take, during our early times together. And I have a sixth sense that the same heavenly angels will guide Charles and Polly too.'

Index

Angelo, Megano – Herero tribal elder, Nxau Nxau, Botswana.
Bazhong Hangheng Plc – Zhang Jinchu's Chinese corporation.
Braunschweig-Lüneberg, Duke Gustav von – Christiane's great-grandfather.
Chen, Alguro – Chinese gemstone smuggler, Namibia.
Clark, Eustace – 1961/62 District Commissioner, N'Gamiland.
Dithopo, Michael – Batauana, founder member, N'Gamiland's FPS.
Duncan, Charles – son of Dr Mathew and Jan.
Duncan, Sir Colin – Charles's grandfather.
Duncan Jan, née Labuschagne – Charles's mother.
Duncan, Mathew, Dr – Charles's father.
Duncan, Sebastian, Major – Charles's uncle.
Eisenberg, Philip – Durham University, visiting research fellow.
Erasmus, Johan – Windhoek National Museum Archives, Namibia.
Freidrich, Ulrich – Okahandja Archives Department, Namibia.
'Gabriel' – Herero, nephew of 'Kisi', Nxau Nxau, Botswana.
Hicks, Barrie – British High Commission, Windhoek, Namibia.
Huang, Benjamin – Chinese gemstone operator, Botswana.
Jinchu, Li Yang – Chinese mineral specialist, Kitwe, Zambia.
Jinchu, Zhang – Li Yang's son, mineral stone dealer, Botswana.
Kakuii – Sam Cohen Library/Archives, Swakopmund, Namibia.
Kandorozu, Jefta – Herero tribal elder, Nxau Nxau, Botswana.
Kay, Robert and June – founder members of N'Gamiland's F.P.S.
Khama, Katsuro – Japanese mineral stone dealer, Botswana.
Kisi – assistant to Chief Moagi Tjamuaha, Nxau Nxau, Botswana.

Klös, Heinz – Police Superintendent, Okahandja, Namibia.
Leutwein, Theodor – Governor of German SW Africa.
Lüneberg, Christiane – Durham Univ. and of Schloss Braunschweig,
Maharero, Samuel – 1904, Paramount Chief, Herero Tribe, SW Africa.
Mothinsi – Herero tribe, Maun, informer for MI6, Botswana.
Ngosi – Nxau Nxau Herero Chief, Moagi Tjamuaha, often addressed.
Ochuros, Esther – murdered niece of Jefta Kandorozu, Nxau Nxau.
Olingo, Daniel – father of Polly and of adopted son, Marcus.
Olingo, Lucienne, née Luzembo – mother of Marcus and Polly.
Olingo, Marcus – son of Lucienne, and adopted son of Daniel.
Otjiherero – Herero language linking Namibia, Botswana and Angola.
Patterson, Colin – British High Commission, Gaberone, Botswana.
Prior, Sam – Professor of Zoology, Durham University.
Ramsden, Jack – Batauana, founder member of N'Gamiland's FPS
Riruako, Thopelo – Herero, senior tribal elder, Nxau Nxau, Botswana.
Riruko, Hosea – Herero, retired tribal chief, Arandis, Namibia.
Sanchuan Huanton Corporation Int. – Li Yang Jinchu's company.
Semmler von, Wolfgang, Count – Christiane Lüneberg's distant cousin.
SWAPO Party – the South West Africa People's Organisation.
Tjipene – Herero, Nxau Nxau. Cousin to Mothinsi in Maun, Botswana.
Tjamuaha, Moagi – chief of the Herero tribe, Nxau Nxau, Botswana.
Tonata –aA prostitute, Maun, Botswana.
'*Vernichtungsbefehl*' – 1904, von Trotha's 'Order of Extermination'.
von Trotha, Lothar, General – 1904–1906, German SW Africa.
Waterberg Battle –1904 Herero and Nama uprising, SW Africa.